Ajay Nair is an award-winning author whose captivating storytelling transcends genres, drawing readers into richly imagined worlds. Born and raised in South India and now residing in Canada, Ajay masterfully weaves narratives that delve into themes of resilience, identity, and societal challenges.

His diverse body of work includes the gripping novel The Woman with Two Shadows, the heartwarming Cutie Fox series (Cutie Fox Stories and Cutie Fox Went to Fiji), and the evocative poetry collection Celestial Poems.

Deeply inspired by his cultural heritage and personal experiences, Ajay's writing shines a light on untold stories and amplifies marginalized voices. Whether crafting enchanting children's adventures, stirring poetry, or suspenseful fiction, his works resonate deeply with readers of all ages, offering both entertainment and thought-provoking insights.

Discover more about Ajay Nair's journey and explore his complete collection of works at www.ajaynairbooks.com.

THE
WOMAN
WITH TWO
SHADOWS

A gripping thriller about revenge, family secrets and betrayal

AJAY NAIR

Every Story has its own Shadows.
(Thanks for being a part of mine

Ajay Nair Books

First published in India by Tridev Publishers, 2024

Internationally published by Author,2025

Copyright © Ajay Nair

Ajay Nair asserts the moral right to be identified as the author of this work.

Dedication

This book is dedicated to the remarkable women who have shaped my life with their strength and determination.

Firstly, to my mother — a true gem whose entire life was a testament to selfless dedication to her family. While she remained unknown to the world at large, she was everything to my world. Like countless mothers, she quietly plays her part in shaping future citizens. I honour her for the life she has enabled me to live and for the boundless love she bestowed upon me.

Secondly, to my wife — a source of constant surprises with her resilience and unwavering commitment to our family. Her passion and devotion serve as a perpetual inspiration, urging me onward. She stands as a role model for young individuals striving to achieve greatness in their lives. I am profoundly grateful to have her by my side, shaping our children's lives with her strength and love.

Lastly, this book also celebrates all the women who steadfastly support their families, often without recognition or reward. They are the unyielding pillars of their households, embodying resilience and sacrifice in ways that deserve our deepest admiration. This book is a tribute to their invaluable contributions and a testament to the power of their influence.

Prologue

Kelu had been living like a king, but today, he was brought down to nothing. He couldn't believe how drastically fate had turned on him.

Surya pushed Kelu and asked him to walk faster towards the outbuilding.

Kelu picked up his pace but did not say a word. His mind was a whirlwind of confusion and betrayal. How had everything changed so quickly? Just yesterday, he had been surrounded by respect and admiration, and now, he was little more than a condemned man, shunned by those he had once commanded.

In the outbuilding, the air was cooler but stale, filled with the faint smell of damp earth and old wood. Cobwebs clung to the corners, and the small, barred window let in just enough light to reveal the dusty remnants of forgotten belongings. It was a place where secrets were buried, and now it would be Kelu's prison, hidden away from prying eyes and the judgment of the villagers.

Surya pushed Kelu inside and locked it. He walked away, saying, 'Old man, stay there and do not try anything tricky. You are lucky Bhavani is keeping you here. I will be back with some food tomorrow.'

As Surya's footsteps moved away, Kelu sat down on the floor and screamed with all his strength, letting out his anger and sadness.

Part One: Lakshmi

Southern India
Late 18th Century

Everyone in the village looked at her as a goddess living on earth—Lakshmi, Kalu's beloved wife. She had beautiful, long, curly hair. A smile never left her face, but her eyes always had an intensity to them. She always dressed fashionably, with lots of jewellery, and she walked with purpose. Everyone respected her.

Lakshmi and Kelu had been married for years, and no one had ever seen them fight. Life was beautiful with their daughter, Narayani, who was totally a daddy's girl. When Kelu was at home, Narayani never left his side. She walked with him and tried to mimic his expressions.

The villagers saw the couple as their Gods and lovingly called them Kelu Thampra and Lakshmi Thampratti.

The couple used their wealth to help those in need, and people from many villages always waited for them at their house, which was known as Vilasam Bungalow.

In India, when a house name ends with the word bungalow, it means it belongs to a rich family. It was the only house in the village with luxurious teakwood sculptures carved in and baked tiles on the roof. Even the king visited their house for rest during his travels.

Kelu was a prominent figure in the village. He was an established businessman who owned many paddy fields and coconut tree fields.

He hailed from a higher-caste family, whose ancestors worked for the king. Once a month, they had village court, and Kelu served as a judge between villagers, who had great faith in his verdicts. Kelu never allowed himself to do anything that could harm the villagers and always saw the best in them.

Kelu wanted his village to differ from others. He wanted to make his village an example for everyone to learn and love people. His became the first village to let women from low caste cover their upper bodies. Many prominent figures did not welcome the move. Even the king came out to see Kelu.

The villagers defended Kalu's decision, saying, 'Our leader is Kelu and we want our women to wear proper clothes and walk without fear in society.'

The king left the village but warned Kelu that this could turn people against him. Kelu just smiled.

There were rumours. Lakshmi was born and brought up in a low-caste family, though this was said hush-hush. No one ever dared ask the couple.

The truth was, Lakshmi was from a low-caste family. Kelu first saw her during his business trips to a nearby village. She was coming from a pond with her friends after her bath. Her thin clothes were wet and stuck to her body, and just like any other low-caste woman, she could not cover her chest. The water from her wet hair dripped onto her breasts, and Kelu couldn't take his eyes away from her beauty. The droplets glowed in the sunset's orange hue.

Lakshmi's skin glistened in the fading light, her smooth, dusky complexion highlighting her high cheekbones and large, expressive eyes. Her wet hair, cascading down her back in dark waves, framed her delicate features perfectly.

As she laughed and chatted with her friends, her full lips curved into a smile that seemed to light up her entire face. Her slender form moved gracefully, each step revealing a natural elegance that captivated Kelu.

Lakshmi was immersed in her own world with her friends, laughing and talking loudly. They were being silly, pushing, pulling each other, and walking without minding where they were going.

Kelu stopped in the middle of the ottayadi patha, a minor road made of mud only wide enough for one-way walking traffic.

Distracted by their banter and play, the girls did not see Kelu and walked into him.

Lakshmi, walking at the front of the group, was jolted by the touch of a man. Her bare breast touched his body.

Kelu held her shoulders and stopped her from falling backward. She didn't know what to do. Terrified, she jumped off the path and down to the field with her friends, and they all kneeled down to the dirty water.

With folded hands, they said, 'Thampra, please forgive us. We never saw you. It was our fault. Please don't punish us.'

Kelu continued on his way and could hear the girls laughing as he walked away. But Lakshmi's beauty stayed with him for many sleepless nights. He kept thinking about her soft body touching his.

He knew society would not accept a relationship between them, and also knew that he could not bring unwelcome attention to his family. He worried his image and the respect he'd earned from the villagers would get ruined.

Still, Kelu wanted to know more about her. He didn't even know her name. All he knew was that she bathed in that pond.

Every night, as he lay in bed, Kelu's mind would wander back to that moment on the ottayadi patha. The memory of her laughter, her unguarded joy, and her striking beauty haunted him.

He felt a strange mixture of guilt and longing, torn between his desires and the harsh realities of society.

The more he thought about her, the stronger his determination grew. He knew he had to see her again, to speak to her, and to find a way to make her a part of his life, despite the insurmountable odds.

After a few days, Kelu could take it no more and went back to that pond. There, he waited for hours, but she did not come. He saw the group of girls she'd been with previously, but she was not with them.

Kelu wanted to ask about her, but he did not have the courage to do so. As he walked away, he saw a girl approaching from the far end of the field.

His heart raced as he waited, hoping she was the one. Then he saw her face—it was her!

As the girl approached the pond, Kelu asked, 'Can I know your name?'

Lakshmi looked up and saw the same man she had run into a few days ago. It terrified her. She knew once a man from a higher caste took interest; they could ruin a girl from a lower caste for life. They could take them away as a servant or use them for sexual pleasures.

She and her friends knew of many instances where men had taken girls and never returned, not even for their parents' deaths.

Usually, those women lived until their beauty faded or the man who took them found another, younger interest. Some became pregnant, but no one ever took them back, not even their own families. Most fed their babies by selling themselves.

All those thoughts raced through Lakshmi's mind, and she turned and ran, dropping her change of clothes on the ground.

'I want to marry you,' Kelu called out to her.

Lakshmi stopped, not believing what she heard. She turned and looked at him again. She wanted to make sure the man was indeed upper caste.

He was walking toward her. Her heart started beating heavily.

Kelu approached her and said, 'I have never seen a beauty like you. I have not slept since the time you touched me. I want to know more about you and your family.'

'Thampra,' she responded, 'please do not give me hopes. I do not know how to dream. I am well aware your caste cannot accept me. Please let me go. I don't want to get into trouble.'

Kelu knew what he wanted would be difficult. Society would be all over them. He also knew the danger—she could be killed. He would be smart not to engage society with this. Still, he wanted to buy some time and get her confidence.

The last thing he wanted was to scare this girl away. He knew he could easily get her to quench his lust by using his power. No one would question him. He could keep her as mistress.

But Kelu did not want to do that. He believed in doing it right. He was a man of principles.

'What is your name?' he asked again.

'Thampra, please leave me alone. Please.' She tried hard not to cry.

'Tell me your name and I will let you go.'

Finally, after a few tries, Lakshmi told him her name.

Kelu loved her name and mentioned it to her. He then asked about her residence and her family's occupation, interested in understanding their caste through their work.

She said her father made gold jewellery, which was something a lower Hindu caste called thattan did.

Kelu hailed from the Nair family, and he knew this would be a colossal problem. Yet, he wanted to make her his bride.

Kelu told her he would come back another day to meet her family.

Lakshmi pleaded with him not to come. She knew her parents would kill her even though she'd done nothing wrong.

Kelu took her hands and felt her trembling with fear. He wanted to console her, to feel her against him. He told her not to worry.

Lakshmi cried. She couldn't speak.

Kelu held her and she looked at him. Her body involuntarily responded to his embrace. It felt right.

Kelu whispered into her ear that she could trust him, and that he would come back for her. He released his embrace, smiled at her, and walked away.

Upon returning to his hometown, Kelu's mind wandered. He couldn't concentrate on his business. He wanted to go back to Lakshmi, but realized it was not a splendid idea to return too soon.

He needed a plan.

Kelu started noting down all the people he could trust. Most of them were business friends, and he started striking names as he began to doubt their true loyalty to him.

Suddenly, he remembered his childhood friend Vinayan, who had recently moved to Lakshmi's village.

He could trust Vinayan. Kelu plotted how to get Vinayan to help.

But what about Lakshmi and her parents? They may not take the chance. They would know that if they get caught, it would mean nothing less than capital punishment.

Kelu may get a fine or lose some business, but for Lakshmi it would be her life.

Kelu decided he would either marry her or die with her. He was on a mission. His plan had many pieces, and all the pieces had to come together in order for the plan to work.

Early the next morning, Kelu went to Lakshmi's village and asked a few people where Vinayan lived. No one knew who Vinayan was, as he'd moved there only recently.

Kelu grew frustrated. He walked in the market aimlessly. Then, he heard a voice.

'Kelappa!'

Only those who knew him from childhood called him Kelappa. No one else had the freedom to be so familiar. He turned around, praying it was Vinayan. No! It was his neighbour, Marakkar.

Marakkar was a man of about fifty years, his age evident in the lines etched across his face and the slight bend in his backbone. His frame was not heavily built, and his movements were marked by a deliberate, almost cautious grace.

He came from a middle-class family, and his clothes reflected this modest upbringing—a simple dhoti paired with a plain cotton shirt.

From a distance, anyone could recognize Marakkar by his distinctive gait and the ever-present red stains around his chin and on his towel, a telltale sign of his habit of chewing betel leaves. The crimson smudges stood out starkly against the white fabric, a peculiar badge he wore daily. Despite his unassuming appearance, there was a certain authority in his voice, a confidence that came from years of experience and the respect he commanded within the community.

Kelu's heart sank a little as he saw Marakkar approaching, the familiar sight of the red stains and the man's slightly stooped posture making it unmistakably clear who it was. He forced a smile, nodding in acknowledgment as Marakkar drew near.

Kelu couldn't believe his neighbour was there. He had to think fast. What could he say? This was not at all good. Kelu needed to get away from this guy as soon as possible. He could not have him tagging along the whole day.

'What a pleasant surprise! How come you are here today?

Marakkar let out a heavy sigh, shaking his head as he spoke. 'Kelu, you won't believe it! I was just here last week, and yet, here I am again. My family has dragged me back for their endless shopping spree for my son's wedding next month. It's driving me crazy!

But at least now I get to spend some time with you amidst all this chaos.'

His frustration lingered in his tone, but a hint of relief washed over his face as he found comfort in Kalu's presence.

'Sorry, brother. I wish I could hang out with you, but I am leaving to go back. I am here to grab some fruits for my travel. My cart is waiting on the other side of the market.'

'You silly bugger. I know you have some side business you don't want me to know about. You are young, buddy, be careful. That's all I have to say. Marakkar said with a laugh.

Kelu did not respond. He left the market in a hurry. Marakkar stood there and watched him go. Kelu could sense his suspicious eyes following him.

Kelu wandered through the entire village, searching desperately for Vinayan. Each passing moment deepened the ache in his heart, and he felt a sense of hopelessness settling in.

Frustrated, he sat on a stone by the roadside, his thoughts drifting back to that fleeting moment with Lakshmi.

It was a brief encounter, he remembered how she had turned around, unaware, and bumped into him.

The warmth of her body brushed against his, an electric moment that left him breathless. Though they had only shared that one instant, her image lingered in his mind—the way her hair glistened with droplets of water and how her laughter intertwined with the melody of the village.

As he sat there, the memory of her gentle smile and the innocence of that moment resonated deeply within him. But amidst these cherished thoughts, he felt an undercurrent of urgency.

Suddenly, it struck him: it was almost the time of day when those girls first bumped into him.

With a surge of determination, he jumped to his feet and ran toward the pond, hoping to perhaps catch a glimpse of Lakshmi once more.

As Kelu approached the entrance of the pond, he noticed that the area was deserted. The silence around him seemed almost unnatural, amplifying his anticipation.

He stood there, rooted to the spot, his eyes scanning the surroundings. The stillness made him uneasy, but he waited patiently, knowing that someone would come.

After a few moments, his vigilance was rewarded when he saw a figure emerging from the distance, steadily walking toward him.

The sight of another person made Kelu anxious, unsure of how to proceed. It felt strange to just stand there and wait, yet he couldn't bring himself to act otherwise.

After a moment's hesitation, he decided to move, thinking it might be less conspicuous to pass by the man and then return.

With his eyes fixed on the ground, Kelu began to walk, deliberately avoiding any eye contact. He wanted to minimize the interaction as much as possible.

As the man drew nearer, Kelu noticed his traditional attire—a simple white mundu wrapped around his waist, the loose end draped over his shoulder. His build was solid but lean, and the lines on his face suggested a life of hard work. In his hands, the man carried pot filled with milk, the aroma faintly drifting through the humid air.

When Kelu was almost close enough to pass, the man suddenly stopped. Kelu hesitated, sensing something familiar in the stranger's stance. As Kelu approached, the man remained still, his eyes focused intently on him.

Finally, the man spoke, his voice filled with a mixture of disbelief and recognition.

'Kelu, is that you?'

Kelu looked up sharply, and his heart skipped a beat. It was Vinayan—Vinay, his old friend. But Kelu needed to be cautious. He had a plan in mind, and it was crucial that Vinay was on board before anyone else, especially before Lakshmi, shows up. Kalu's mind raced as he considered his options.

Without saying a word, he reached out and grabbed Vinay's hand, pulling him toward a nearby bush. Vinay, caught off guard, stumbled, and the pot of milk he was carrying tipped over, spilling its contents onto the ground. The white liquid soaked into the earth, a wasted sacrifice.

'What's going on, Kelu?' Vinay demanded; his voice tinged with irritation as he regained his balance. He glanced at the spilled milk with a frown, clearly upset by the loss.

Kelu told Vinay he was in the village for something important, something he could not do without Vinay's help.

Knowing Kelu was from a wealthy family and didn't need anybody's help—he could simply order his workers to do things—Vinay knew this must be something very important, and special.

They heard some girls coming, preceded by their laughing and singing. Kelu's face changed. His sullen face blushed, revealing his feelings.

Vinay realized Kalu's 'something' had to do with the girls who were approaching. He peeked out to see the girls and saw that none of them were from the upper caste. He was puzzled about what Kelu wanted from him, and what help he needed.

Vinay, his patience wearing thin, shook Kelu by the shoulders, his frustration bubbling over. 'You dragged me here, and now I've spilled the milk meant for my family! And all you can do is stand there, staring at those low-caste girls? What's going on with you?'

Kelu's eyes flared with anger. He jerked away from Vinay's grip, his voice trembling with a mix of fury and something deeper.

'They are people like us, Vinay! Don't you dare call them low caste!'

Vinay was taken aback, unable to process what he had just heard. This was not the Kelu he knew—the Kelu who had once sneered at those of lower castes, who had thrown stones at their huts with other boys, laughing at their plight.

Back in their school days, Kelu had always been the one to make cruel jokes about the low-caste people, seeing them as less than human, unworthy of respect. He had relished the divide that society had ingrained in them, mocking those who were born into a life of hardship and servitude.

But now, standing before him, was a Kelu who spoke with a conviction that seemed alien. Vinay could see the struggle in Kelu's eyes, the turmoil of a man who was confronting the very beliefs he had once held so dear. It was as if Kelu was at war with himself, trying to reconcile the prejudice of his past with the compassion that was now surfacing within him.

Kelu's face hardened, his jaw set with determination. 'You don't understand, Vinay. Things are different now. I'm different now.

Vinay could hardly believe his ears. This was not just a sudden change of heart; it was a complete upheaval of everything Kelu had once stood for.

Vinay felt a pang of confusion and anger, struggling to grasp how his friend could have shifted so drastically. 'What happened to you, Kelu? Where's the man I used to know?'

But Kelu had no answer, at least none that he could easily put into words. The truth was, he didn't fully understand it himself. Kelu didn't know where to begin, or how to explain. At last, he got some courage.

'Vinay, I am so sorry to come across harshly. I need a huge favor. This is very dangerous, but please do not say no.'

Vinay stared at Kelu, impatient for him to continue.

'I like one girl in that group. I have never seen such a beauty before.'

Vinay laughed. 'So, what's the problem? You are a rich man. Talk to her father, give him some money, and take her as your housemaid. You could do as you wish. Everyone does this. I am sure your family has been doing this for many years. Don't tell me you have never done something like this before.'

Kelu wanted to slap Vinay for saying that, but he needed his help badly and knew there was no one else he could trust. He looked at the girls, who were having a splendid time, then turned back to Vinay.

'Vinay, I am in love with her. I want to marry her and I need your help. I have a plan, but in order for the plan to work, I need your entire family to play a part. I cannot trust anyone else with this.'

'Are you out of your mind? Do you know what would happen to your family, and mine? I will not play any part in this. Unlike you, I do not have the means to take care of my family. You have money and a great reputation. You can do whatever you want, but leave me alone. You are on your own, my friend.' Vinay grabbed his empty milk container and started to leave.

Kelu grabbed his hand and begged. 'Please don't go. Just hear me out. I have no one here to help and you are my friend. Please stop and listen to me.'

Vinay took a deep breath, his chest rising and falling as he struggled to steady himself. 'Alright, I'll listen to what you have to say. I owe you that much. You fed me when I had nothing at school, when I was too ashamed to admit that I couldn't afford even a handful of rice. I haven't forgotten your kindness, Kelu. But understand this—I'm not a rich man like you. My family depends on me, and I can't afford to get caught up in whatever madness you are planning. For you, this might be just another adventure, something to break the monotony. You have the king's favour, and if things go wrong, you can walk away unscathed. But me? I could lose everything. I might even lose my life.'

Vinay's words hung in the air, heavy with the weight of his fears and insecurities. His life had never been easy. As a labourer, he managed other low-caste workers, a job that paid just enough to keep his family from starving but not enough to lift them out of poverty.

The caste system had closed every door to him, denying him any opportunity for advancement.

He had no education, no skills beyond what was needed to survive day by day. His move to this new land had been a desperate attempt to start over, but the struggle to make ends meet had followed him like a shadow.

He looked at Kelu, his eyes searching for any sign of understanding. 'This isn't some game for me, Kelu. I can't just pick up the pieces and move on if things go south. My family... they need me. And if I get involved in this, I might not be around to provide for them. You have to understand that.'

Kelu saw the fear in Vinay's eyes, the desperation of a man who had nothing left to lose except the fragile stability he had managed to carve out for himself.

The realization hit him hard—this wasn't just about him or his plans. It was about the lives of people like Vinay, who had so little to begin with.

Kelu softened his tone, trying to convey the sincerity of his intentions.

'Vinay, I promise you this—nothing will happen to you. I will make sure of it. You won't be in danger, and I will help you with money. If anything goes wrong and you lose your job because of this, I will take care of you. I'll set you up with my business, and you won't have to worry about your family's future.'

Vinay's expression wavered, the tension in his face slowly easing as he considered Kelu's words. Kelu had always been a man of his word, and despite his reservations, Vinay felt a flicker of hope.

The thought of securing a better future for his family, of finally breaking free from the chains of his current existence, was tempting. He knew Kelu's influence and resources could change his life.

'Alright, Kelu,' Vinay said, his voice calmer now, though still tinged with uncertainty. 'Tell me your plan. I'll hear you out. But remember—I'm putting my trust in you. Don't let me down.'

'I need you to move from this village.'

'What? Move from here? I just started my life here. I am going now, you are insane.'

Kelu grabbed Vinay's arms, begging. 'Please show some mercy and hear me out fully. I will take care of you for all the trouble. I cannot live without her. Please listen.'

Vinay sat back down. 'Okay, go on. I'm listening.'

'I need you and your family to move far away from this village. We need to convince Lakshmi's parents to do the same, come with you to the same village. Once they leave this village, I want them to act like a higher-caste family. You need to take them to your new house and get them introduced to others in the new village as your close relatives.'

Vinay shot up from the ground. 'There is no way Savitri will go along with this. She will not have a low caste inside her house. Besides, she knows everyone, even the distant relatives, in my family.'

'Vinay, you just agree; I will get Savitri on board for me. She will do it. I am sure of it.'

Vinay paused, his mind a jumble of thoughts. He was not sure how this would play out. He knew low-caste people talked different slang than higher-caste people did. That, itself, was a huge issue.

There was a lot of preparation to do. They would have to learn the customs and behaviours of the higher caste. How was that going to happen?

Even a minor mistake could expose everyone, leading to a revolt. The community would riot. People could die. Kelu was not thinking properly. He stared at Kelu without saying a word.

Kelu grabbed Vinay by the shoulders and shook him gently but with urgency. 'Come on, man, please say yes. You have to trust me on this one—there's a lot more to this plan than you realize. Once you hear it out fully, I'm sure you'll feel more confident.'

Vinay sighed deeply; his face lined with the weight of years of hard living. 'Enough of your plans, brother. You know how to convince me; that's not the problem. But what about Savitri? You'll need to convince her too, and that's a whole different story. And it's not just her—you've got to convince the girl's family as well. Do you really think everyone is going to fall in line and dance to your tune? If that's what you're expecting, you're out to lunch. But listen,' he paused, glancing down at the dusty ground as if searching for the right words, 'I owe you a lot, so I'll help you. But I have one condition: you must promise me, Kelu, that you'll take care of Savitri and my son, Kannan.'

Vinay's thoughts drifted for a moment as he considered his family. He had been married to Savitri for eight years now. They had met when they were both young, their union arranged by their families, a marriage forged not in love but in necessity and survival.

Over the years, their bond had deepened through shared struggles and quiet moments of understanding. Kannan, their son, was just five years old, a bright and curious child who was the light of Vinay's life.

The thought of leaving them unprotected gnawed at him, but he knew he had little choice. This life had given him few options, and he needed to secure their future, whatever it took.

'I'm serious, Kelu,' Vinay continued, his voice taking on a rough edge, 'I need your word. Savitri and Kannan—they are my world. If anything happens to me, they must be cared for. That's the only way I can go along with whatever you're planning. Do you understand?'

Kelu looked into Vinay's eyes, seeing the gravity of his friend's request. He nodded solemnly, realizing the depth of responsibility that came with Vinay's condition. The plan might have started as a scheme, but now it carried the weight of lives and futures.

Kelu hugged him hard and laughed.

'I will buy you land in the village so you can move and set up a small shop for your beloved Savitri. I am happy already. I know I can convince rest of them. I will rule this world, man.'

'Wait. Moving is fine, but what is the actual plan after that? Say everyone including girl's family are on board. Then what?'

'You stay in the new village for six months. Make others believe this family is your relatives. Get them to behave like us. Teach our language, how to walk, dress and conduct business like us. After six months, you come to my village and bring them to my family as a wedding proposal for me. But, when you come to my village, you introduce them as your family friends and business partner. No one will question you by that time. Six months is plenty enough to get them ready. I am sure Savitri can play a monumental part on this.'

'Plan's not bad,' Vinay said. 'I like it. But if Savitri is not on board, please do not blame or force me. If I was alone, I would do this for you with no hesitation.'

'Done,' Kelu confidently said. He was sure everybody else would follow the plan.

Kelu looked up toward the sky, and he felt like thanking the universe.

They heard the girls again, headed back after their bath.

Vinay asked, 'Who is this girl who stole your heart? Show me.'

'Come, let's go toward them.'

Kelu started walking, and Vinay followed. He found it hard to keep up with Kelu, who was not walking but closer to running. The girls came up the ottayadi patha and Kelu saw Lakshmi leading the pack. He gleamed, and his heart pounded.

Kelu said, 'Look. The girl coming at the front with her hair tied above her forehead is the one.'

Vinay realized why Kelu was head over heels for her. The tallest and lightest-skinned among them, she really was a goddess. Her skin had a glow, and the setting sun made her even more delightful to look at.

Vinay noticed Kelu looking at him, and they smiled at each other.

Vinay playfully punched Kelu's stomach. 'Now I know now why you want to put all of us on our deathbed. Well, I think it's worth the risk. Let's see what Savitri has to say.'

Lakshmi saw Kelu and stepped back. She asked the other girls to keep her in the middle of the group.

Kelu asked Vinay to step off the ottayadi patha so the girls could pass. This was the first time this had happened. It's always the low caste who step aside so the higher caste can walk.

Lakshmi looked at Kelu while walking. Their eyes met. Kelu told her with his eyes he was coming for her. She had a smile on her face, but her eyes were scared.

Kelu wanted to say don't worry, but the other girls pushed her and asked her to walk faster. They all giggled as they passed.

'It's getting late,' Kelu said. 'Let's go buy milk and go home. I will stay with you tonight. You tell Savitri that you met me on the way and got late. Let's hurry now.'

Vinay was worried, but he did not show that to Kelu. He walked silently with Kelu, who kept talking and talking. Vinay did not pay attention, his mind adrift. Then he felt a hand on his shoulder.

'This is the shop, isn't it?' Kelu asked. 'Where are you going? Get the milk and let's go home. I am eager to get the plan going with Savitri.'

Vinay realized Savitri was not expecting anybody with him, so it would be wise to get some food. They got what they needed, Kelu paid for everything, and they hurried back.

As they approached, he saw Savitri pacing in front of the house. She seemed worried.

'Savitri's not in a pleasant mood,' Vinay told Kelu. 'I'm late, and Kannan must be hungry. I think today we should say nothing about the plan.'

Kelu wouldn't listen.

As Savitri saw Vinay and Kelu approaching from a distance, she quickly called out to Kannan, her five-year-old son, who was playing with a stick in the dirt near the small, thatched hut they called home.

'Kannan, come inside,' she said with a mix of urgency and irritation in her voice.

The child looked up, sensing his mother's tension, and obediently ran toward her.

When Vinay and Kelu finally arrived at the entrance to their humble home, Savitri greeted them both, forcing a polite smile onto her tired face.

The house was a modest structure, built from sunbaked mud and wood, with a roof thatched from dried coconut leaves.

The walls were weathered and cracked in places, evidence of the many monsoons they had endured. There was no door, just a simple cloth hung in the entrance to offer some privacy.

Inside, the space was sparse, with only the most basic necessities—a few pots and pans, a small fire pit for cooking, and a mat on the floor where they slept.

As she stood in the doorway, Savitri's appearance reflected the hard life she had lived. Her sari, once a deep shade of indigo, had faded to a dull gray from countless washes in the river. The edges were frayed, and it clung to her thin frame, a testament to their ongoing struggle with poverty.

Her skin was darkened by the relentless sun, toughened by years of labour in the fields and by the cooking fire. Her hands were calloused, fingers roughened from pulling weeds, washing clothes, and grinding grains.

Deep lines etched across her forehead and around her eyes, and there was a hint of sadness in her gaze—a reflection of the burdens she carried daily.

When her eyes met Vinay's, there was a flash of frustration and disappointment, barely concealed beneath her forced hospitality. He was late again. But with Kelu present, she could not say what she truly felt, so she bit her tongue and kept her thoughts to herself.

Instead, she reached out with an abrupt movement and snatched the food packet and the small container of milk from Vinay's hands, her actions speaking louder than words.

Without another word, she turned and disappeared into the hut, leaving the men to their own company.

Vinay and Kelu exchanged a knowing glance, a faint smile playing on their lips as they both understood Savitri's unspoken words.

Vinay felt a pang of guilt as he watched her retreat into the house. He knew she was upset with him for being late, for the many times he had come home empty-handed, and for the life of hardship they led. But what could he say? He was a man with few options, doing the best he could with what little he had.

They settled down on the verandah, a simple raised platform made of packed earth and wooden beams that extended out from the front of the hut. It was their usual spot, a place where they could sit and talk, looking out at the patch of land that surrounded their home.

The evening light was beginning to fade, casting long shadows across the ground, and the sound of cicadas filled the air. Kannan, now clinging to his mother's leg inside the hut, peeked out from behind her, his wide eyes watching the two men with curiosity.

As they sat, the air was thick with unspoken words and shared understanding.

Savitri, though out of sight, remained on Vinay's mind. He could sense her frustration, the weight of their shared struggles, and he wished he could do more to ease her burden. But for now, all he could do was sit beside Kelu, sharing a moment of respite before the weight of the world returned.

'Kelu, it has been a long time,' Savitri called out. 'How are you doing these days? Shall I make tea for you?'

'Savitri, it's already time for dinner. Let's eat, then we can have tea and talk,' Kelu said as he smirked at Vinay. In return, Vinay mimed hanging himself. They both laughed.

Kannan came out a few minutes later. He'd had his shower, and his forehead had sandalwood paste.

Seeing the sandalwood paste, Kelu said, 'You prayed. Righteous son. It is always nice to see a youngster like you still following our heritage. Pray daily, son. We get busy and never find time to pray.'

Kannan, a bright-eyed five-year-old with oiled hair and a mischievous grin, looked up at his father with a mix of relief and disappointment. His small hands fiddled with the hem of his worn-out shirt, a garment that had seen better days, now patched in several places by his mother's careful hand.

'Father, you're lucky your friend came with you,' Kannan said in a soft, slightly pouty voice.

'Mother wasn't happy earlier, but she seems better now that Uncle Kelu is here.'

He glanced at his father with a hint of sadness in his eyes, his voice dropping to a whisper. 'But I'm not happy now. I wanted to play with you, but it's already bedtime. You promised we'd play tomorrow, right?'

Kannan's words carried the innocent honesty of a child, his small body leaning against the doorframe as he spoke.

Though young, Kannan was already aware of the moods that swirled around him, sensing his mother's earlier frustration and now feeling the weight of his own disappointment.

All he wanted was a few moments with his father before the night drew to a close, to share in the simple joys of playing together. But the day had slipped away too quickly, and now the promise of tomorrow was all he had to cling to.

Vinay hugged him and gave him a kiss. 'We will play tomorrow I promise. Now go to bed as a good boy.'

Kannan turned to Kelu. 'Uncle, good night.' He ran inside.

'Son, eat before you go to bed,' Vinay yelled.

'I fed already. Do you think I would make him starve all this time while you and your friend were outside having fun?'

Vinay didn't say a word. They all washed their hands and sat down. Kelu looked at Vinay and raised his eyebrows.

Savitri noticed the awkward silence hanging in the air as they sat together on the verandah. The quiet was unusual, especially with Kelu around. She stepped out of the hut, carrying a simple meal of rice and lentils, and set it down in front of the men. The firelight flickered on her weary face, softening the hard lines etched by years of labour.

'Come, eat,' she said, her voice gentle but firm, though her eyes darted between the two men. She could feel something was off, something unspoken lingering between them.

As they began to eat in silence, Savitri couldn't hold back any longer.

'What's going on?' she asked, her tone a mix of curiosity and concern. 'Why are you both so quiet? Is everything okay?'

She paused, then turned directly to Kelu, who was usually full of stories whenever he visited. 'Kelu, can you at least tell me what's happening? It's been so long since we've seen you, and now you show up without any warning. I'm all ears here.'

Vinay glanced at Kelu, signalling with a slight nod that it was time to start talking.

Kelu took a deep breath, trying to gauge how to ease into the conversation without overwhelming Savitri.

'We'll get to that, Savitri,' Kelu began cautiously, placing some rice into his mouth to buy a moment of thought.

He looked at her, noticing the exhaustion in her eyes but also the strength that had carried her through so many hardships. 'But first, tell me—how has everything been here? How's Kannan doing in the village school?'

Savitri sighed, her tension momentarily easing as she spoke about their son. 'Kannan is doing well, though he's restless. He asks about his father all the time and misses him when he's away. But you didn't answer my question, Kelu. What brings you here after all this time?'

Kelu exchanged another glance with Vinay, understanding that there was no avoiding it now. He carefully chose his words, not wanting to alarm her but also needing to be honest.

'Savitri, we've been talking about something important. It's a plan we've been working on, something that could change our lives—especially Vinay's and yours. But it's risky, and I wanted to make sure Vinay understood everything before we brought it up to you.'

Savitri's eyes narrowed slightly as she tried to read Kelu's expression. The fact that they were being so careful with their words made her uneasy. 'A plan? What kind of plan?' she asked, her voice now tinged with worry.

Kelu hesitated, glancing at the food in front of him, He knew that what he said next would set the tone for the entire conversation.

'It's something that could help us, Savitri. It's not easy to explain, but I promise you, it's meant to secure a better future for all of us. I just need you to trust us.'

As he spoke, Kelu couldn't help but think about the weight of the plan they were about to unfold. It was bold, perhaps even dangerous, but in their desperate situation, it felt like the only chance they had.

He only hoped that when Savitri heard the full story, she would see the necessity of it, even if it filled her with the same anxiety that Vinay had already shown.

Without taking a single breath, Kelu explained his plan.

Vinay kept his head down and his mouth full of food.

When Kelu finished speaking, a few minutes passed in silence. No one said a word.

Kelu glanced at Vinay, who still hadn't looked up from his plate.

Savitri continued eating, her expression neutral. She even asked Kelu to pass her more food from the pot near him.

Kelu and Vinay exchanged puzzled looks. The room felt heavy with unspoken words. The clinking of utensils was the only sound, amplifying the tension.

Vinay was engulfed in a whirlpool of anxiety. He was torn between his loyalty to his friend and the fear of the consequences they might face.

He kept his gaze down, hoping to avoid any confrontation for the moment. His thoughts were consumed with the complexities of their plan and the potential fallout if things went wrong.

Savitri, seemingly calm, knew Vinay well enough to sense his unease and could see the urgency in Kelu's eyes. She chose to maintain a facade of normalcy, hoping to diffuse the situation.

Then, Savitri abruptly stopped eating. She looked up, determined, and said, 'Plan's good. I will do it, but on one condition.'

'What?' Kelu asked.

'Land and store all good. I'll take that. But Kelu also takes responsibility Kannan's education.'

Vinay looked at Savitri with anger and started to speak. Vinay's eyes widened with anger. He stared at Savitri, his frustration boiling over. 'Savitri, this is too much. You can't just—'

'You stay out of this,' Savitri said. 'This is my house and I am taking a huge risk here. You could get killed, and I want my son's future secured. You could never give him the education Kelu can provide for our son. He has the means to support it.'

Savitri turned to Kelu. 'This is the only reason I am agreeing to this plan.' Savitri got up and took the plates from the floor. She started to go inside, then stopped and looked back. 'Just keep that in both of your minds. I am doing this for my son. Period.'

With those words hanging in the air, she turned and walked inside, leaving Kelu and Vinay to contemplate the weight of her commitment and the sacrifices she was willing to make for their family's future.

Kelu broke into laughter. 'You are very lucky, Vinay, to have a wife like this who has real backbone. Look at her, how quickly she put both of us in our place. I liked her business acumen. You need to learn a lot from your wife, man. Tell her I am okay with her condition. Forget about this house and from now on you will live like a king.'

'Lucky my foot. Try living with her. Don't worry, you are in love. You will see soon how that turns out after marriage.'

Kelu laughed.

Vinay went inside. Savitri was in the kitchen emptying the dishes. Vinay touched her shoulder. She looked at him and said, 'Kelu is crazy. He might die over this. We have to be very careful. If something happens, put everything on his head. Don't fight me. I know he's your friend, but family comes first. Don't make me say this again. I want that store in my name. Go out there and tell him to fulfil all his promises before we just get up and leave this town.'

Vinay could see the determination on her face.

For a second, Vinay had hoped Savitri would refuse to participate and all this trouble would go away.

Now, it was a comprehensive plan and everyone needed to play their part well.

'Are you going to say something to him,' Savitri said, 'or do you want me to do that too?'

Vinay found that harsh, but he understood Savitri's point. He was amazed by her willpower, and he realized his family would survive with her even if he was not around. He walked back to the verandah with a spring in his step. He was happy for his family, and also for his childhood friend Kelu.

Kelu was sitting on the step and looking up at the sky. Vinay could see Kelu's worry had diminished. He was happy. Vinay sat beside him.

'Kelu, you are a lucky man. I've never convinced Savitri to do anything before. Now you need to deliver, my friend. She told me she'll move anywhere you want, but you must set up that store first. She wants everything in her name. Can you make it happen?'

'Brother Vinay, you are so trusting. I understand why she wants that done. I am a businessman. I can do that in a week. You get ready for the move. Now, do me a favour. Leave me alone to dream.'

Vinay went inside and came back with bedding. Savitri helped arrange the bedding on the floor so that Kelu could sleep.

'Don't dream too much,' Vinay told Kelu, his voice heavy with weariness. 'Tomorrow, I must work. I cannot waste time sitting around. Leave whenever you like; Savitri will make sure you have food for your journey back.' His words were practical, but the strain in his eyes revealed more than he was willing to share.

Kelu remained silent, lost in his own thoughts, staring blankly at the flickering lamp. The air was thick with unsaid words, tension simmering beneath the surface.

As the night deepened, Vinay and Savitri sat together, their quiet whispers echoing through the small, dimly lit room. They talked endlessly, their minds spinning with worry and hope.

Every detail of their plan for Kelu's return and what lay ahead was meticulously discussed, yet both knew that plans could crumble under the weight of fate.

Savitri's brows furrowed, her eyes glistening with unshed tears, while Vinay's hands trembled slightly as he held her close, feeling the unspoken burden they both carried.

Savitri's voice broke through the silence, gentle but determined. 'Don't worry, Vinay,' she whispered, her fingers brushing away a tear from his cheek. 'Think nothing negative. This is God's will for Kannan. Our son is blessed, and I am certain we will succeed, no matter the cost. This is for our future, for Kannan's future. We have to believe it.'

Her words were meant to soothe, but a trace of doubt lingered in the quiver of her lips.

Vinay tightened his grip around her, drawing strength from the warmth of her embrace. 'I just want to make sure it all goes well, Savitri. I can't afford to fail—not again.'

His voice cracked as he spoke, revealing the fear he desperately tried to hide. They held each other in silence, each drawing comfort from the other's presence, knowing that their hope and faith were the only things keeping them afloat in this storm.

They finally parted with a tight hug, clinging to one another as if to hold on to their shared resolve.

The night stretched on, the weight of their decision pressing down on them, but in the quiet of their togetherness, they found a flicker of hope to carry them through the uncertainty that awaited them with the dawn.

When Vinay went outside the next morning, Kelu was not there. He'd left already, telling no one.

Vinay told Savitri, 'That rascal left already without a word.'

'Good. I don't have to cook food for him.'

Vinay looked at her, annoyed.

She smiled back and continued her work.

As Vinay watched her, he thought her beauty had only increased with age, even though her butt was a little fuller. He also felt the air of joy around her. He went to her and patted her butt. She playfully pushed him away and walked toward Kannan's Room.

Kelu's plan would start in a village called Pala. He chose Pala because no one from his town ever went there, as Pala did not have many businesses.

Kelu portrayed himself as a servant whose job it was to secure a shop for his master to open a clothing store. He asked around to find a suitable store.

Kelu wanted a spot where the store would be in a prime location to have as many interactions as possible.

Finally, after three days of searching, he found the perfect location. The storefront faced the only market and had living quarters.

Kelu put down the advance and said he would bring the family back for the rest of the paperwork.

Finally, Kelu went back home. His family had many questions, as he rarely was away for so long without telling them.

'You guys know Vinay, right?'

'Yes, we know him. What happened?'

'Nothing happened. He's starting a new business in Pala. I'm helping him and I got stuck there. I'll need to go back for two weeks next week.' Kelu excused himself, happy he'd planted the seed that Vinay was starting a business.

Kelu arranged for garments from many cities to arrive at Pala. He wanted to make sure the opening would create a big hype so the townspeople would believe the family was rich.

He went to Pala and made sure everything was in order, even paying to have notices of the grand opening distributed via bullock cart operators. Kelu wanted everything to be perfect.

In all his planning for the shop, Kelu suddenly realized he had yet to talk to Lakshmi's family. His happiness faded. He'd done a lot within a few days but could not fail now.

He went to Vinay's house, only to find no one there. He was furious. He settled in to wait.

Around six o'clock, Savitri got home with Kannan and saw Kelu on the verandah. 'When did you arrive?' she asked.

'Where were you?' Kelu asked angrily. 'I've been waiting all afternoon. I am paying you, and I expect you to be here when I come.'

Savitri told Kannan to go inside. 'Kelu, we may be poor, but we are not your servants or slaves. You want our help then you need to work with us. If you tell us you're coming a certain time we will wait, but we cannot stay home and wait for you every day. We have our lives. Kannan goes to school. He has many things to do. I will not stop my child from living his life.'

Kelu knew he was not helping the situation and apologized to Savitri. He told her he was tense and concerned about talking to Lakshmi's family.

Savitri sat him down. 'Kelu, my husband may be very naïve, but trust me, he can convince anyone. He'll help when you meet with the family.'

Kelu realized that Savitri loved Vinay deeply, and that she trusted him. For a moment, he looked at Savitri and saw her beauty, but then felt bad for looking at her like that. She was like his sister.

Savitri spoke. 'Here comes the useless guy, my man.'

Kelu looked up and saw Vinay coming, carrying milk as usual.

Kelu looked back at Savitri. A few seconds ago, she was praising Vinay, and look at her now—calling him useless.

He hoped Lakshmi was not like this, though he'd heard his mom talking about his father like this, too. All women were the same; they could play the part they needed depending on the tune.

Vinay gave the milk to Savitri, who hurried to the kitchen. Vinay sat down and took his shirt off. 'It was a rough day at work, my friend. I can't wait to get to the shop so I can just sit and sell clothes.'

Kelu did not like that comment. 'Business is difficult. You must work at it. I am only setting this up for you. The rest is in your hands. I'm sure Savitri will straighten you out.'

Kelu told Vinay they had to go to Lakshmi's house the following evening. Vinay was worried. He was not sure how Lakshmi's father would take things.

They ate supper in silence, the weight of the upcoming visit pressing heavily on them. Afterward, everyone retired for the night, though Vinay and Savitri lay awake, unable to sleep.

In the quiet darkness, Savitri turned to Vinay. 'I want Kelu to finalize the business paperwork tomorrow in my name,' she said firmly. 'I need that settled before you go to Lakshmi's house.'

Vinay nodded, understanding her desire for security. 'Okay my boss,' he laughed and hugged his wife. He kissed her forehead and said, 'You can also join us.'

Savitri smiled and agreed to go with them.

At breakfast the next morning, Savitri told Kelu about their decision. Kelu did not object, and they went to Pala as soon as they finished their meal.

Kelu showed them the shop and introduced them to the agent as the shop's owners. They registered the shop in Savitri's name. Savitri was visibly excited, her face glowing with anticipation.

However, Kelu and Vinay remained preoccupied, their thoughts consumed by the impending visit to Lakshmi's house that evening.

'Come on,' Kelu said, 'we need to go back. I want to get it over with.'

'Yes,' Savitri said, 'and school will be releasing Kannan in a few hours as well.'

They picked Kannan up, and he was thrilled to see his father, mother and Kelu uncle together. They went to a tea stall and ate banana fritters with tea.

Kannan was overjoyed, as he usually only got this kind of luxury on Onam festival days.

Kelu got up to pay the shopkeeper and indicated the others should get up as well.

Kannan was still eating, so Kelu said, 'Come on, guys, pack that up for Kannan. He can finish on the way there.'

Savitri did not like that at all, but she knew time was of the essence, so she obliged.

They asked the shopkeeper for directions to Nanu thattan's house, as it was common for people to use their caste as their last name.

Nanu's house was a tiny hut with a coconut leaf thatched roof. The clay walls were cracked and in disrepair. There were no windows, only the frames.

At the entrance was a Tulsi plant. Most Hindu houses had one of these plants, believed to be an earthly manifestation of the goddess Tulsi. Devotees usually put on an oil lamp when the sun sets.

Many coconut leaves were in front of the hut, the roof only half braided. Kelu realized they were changing out the roof. He saw a man in his eighties working on the roof.

'Where can we find Nanu thattan?' Kelu called out.

The man on the roof, Nanu, squinted down at Kelu through the sun's harsh glare. His skin was weathered, darkened from years of labour under the unrelenting skies. He wore a simple loincloth, tied just below his stomach, and his hair was unkempt, sticking out in uneven tufts.

'Thampra, it's me,' he called out, wiping sweat from his brow. 'If you want me to craft some ornaments, I must tell you it will take time. My roof is leaking badly, and I need to patch it before the rains arrive. My apologies.'

Kelu's expression darkened, but he swallowed his impatience. 'Come down. I need to talk to you,' he barked, his tone sharp with a hint of urgency.

Savitri shot Kelu a warning glance, her brows knitting together. She didn't like the roughness in his voice—this was delicate business, and Kelu's impatience could jeopardize everything.

Vinay, sensing the tension, leaned closer and muttered to Kelu, 'Be polite. Remember why we're here. This isn't just about you.'

Nanu, now acutely aware of the importance of the situation, clambered down from the roof with nimble movements that belied his age.

As he approached, he wiped his hands on his threadbare cloth and folded them in a respectful greeting. His feet were calloused, and his clothes, though clean, were old and worn from countless washes. The scent of metal and smoke clung to him, a reminder of his craft as a thattan, a humble goldsmith of the lowest caste.

'Thampra, please forgive me,' Nanu said, bowing slightly. 'I have no fine furniture for you to sit on, only this dusty floor.'

His voice quivered with humility, but there was a steadiness in his gaze, as if he was ready to bear whatever was coming.

His weathered face, lined with years of struggle and survival, betrayed a quiet dignity despite the situation.

Kelu felt a knot tighten in his stomach. His plan was bold, and he knew it would take all the persuasion he could muster to convince Nanu. The weight of the moment pressed on him, making his palms sweat.

This was no ordinary proposal—it involved Lakshmi, Nanu's daughter. How could he convey the significance of his intentions while navigating the rigid caste boundaries that divided them?

Vinay and Savitri exchanged glances, both aware of the delicate ground they were treading on. This was not just a negotiation; it was a clash of tradition, status, and hope for something different.

As Nanu stood there, waiting with bated breath, Kelu realized that his next words could either build a bridge or deepen the divide that separated their worlds.

'Don't worry about that,' Kelu replied. 'We are all okay. I am here because I have a proposition for you.'

Nanu listened intently as Kelu laid out his proposal, his words carefully chosen but laced with a determination that couldn't be missed.

Kelu explained his desire to marry Lakshmi and shared his vision for how they could make this union possible, despite the enormous risks.

Nanu's face remained expressionless, but his eyes flickered with anxiety as Kelu spoke of defying societal norms.

The old man's hands trembled slightly as he gripped the edge of his faded cloth, nervously twisting it as Kelu finished speaking.

When Kelu paused, waiting for a response, Nanu's shoulders slumped in defeat. 'Thampra,' he began, his voice heavy with desperation, 'please, spare us. We are living as happily as we can within our means and do not want to invite any trouble. Society would destroy us if they discovered our low caste. They would not spare my family. Lakshmi is my youngest child, the joy of my heart, and I have three others to care for. We all carry dreams in our hearts—simple dreams, dreams of survival, of living peacefully. Please, Thampra, do not crush those dreams.'

His voice cracked, and tears welled in his tired eyes. Nanu fell at Kelu's feet, sobbing uncontrollably. 'Let us live in peace, Thampra,' he pleaded.

The desperation in his voice echoed in the small room, making even the walls seem to shrink under the weight of his plea.

Kelu stiffened, unsure of how to react. He could feel the sharp gazes from within the house—the shadows of Nanu's other children peeking out from behind the tattered curtain, Lakshmi's eyes among them.

Outside, too, curious neighbours had gathered, drawn by the unfamiliar presence of a higher-caste visitor.

Though they couldn't hear the conversation, the tension was palpable, and Kelu was acutely aware of the weight of his every move.

He wanted to comfort the old man, to assure him that he meant no harm, but he hesitated. Touching a man of lower caste would violate the rigid social boundaries he had grown up with, boundaries that even in this critical moment, he was reluctant to cross.

Before the silence could stretch any further, Savitri stepped forward, her face calm but resolute. 'Kelu, step aside,' she said softly but firmly.

She then knelt beside Nanu 'You listen to me,' she said in a soothing tone, speaking words too low for Kelu to catch.

Her voice was kind, almost maternal, and as she spoke, Nanu's sobs gradually subsided.

Whatever she said to him, it reached the deepest corners of his heart, easing his fears and softening the resistance that had been so firmly etched on his face.

After a few moments, Nanu nodded slowly, wiping his tears on his sleeve. He rose shakily to his feet, giving Savitri a long, searching look before backing away.

Savitri returned to Kelu with a quiet confidence. 'Don't worry,' she said calmly, her eyes gleaming with satisfaction. 'They'll be ready by tomorrow morning for the move.'

Kelu blinked in disbelief. 'How did you manage that?' he asked, unable to mask his surprise.

It had taken him so much time and effort to come up with a plan, yet Savitri had achieved in minutes what he feared would take hours or days.

Savitri simply smiled, her lips curving in that mysterious way women sometimes do when they know more than they let on.

'From today onwards, respect women. We have our ways,' she said, a playful spark in her eyes.

But she offered no further explanation, leaving Kelu to wonder what exactly had passed between her and Nanu in those few minutes.

As she turned to walk away, Kelu caught a glimpse of Lakshmi standing in the doorway, her eyes wide and filled with both fear and hope.

Their gazes met, and for a brief moment, everything else seemed to fade away.

Lakshmi's eyes held a silent question, a mix of gratitude and doubt as she tried to understand the depth of Kelu's intentions.

Kelu felt his heart pound in his chest, knowing that all his plans, his struggles, and his defiance of tradition were for her—for a chance at a future together.

He wanted to assure her that everything would be alright, that he would stand by her no matter what.

Lakshmi, sensing his unspoken promise, offered a small, fleeting smile—a smile that held a world of emotions neither of them could put into words.

Savitri noticed the silent exchange and smirked to herself, but she said nothing.

As they prepared to leave, the air was thick with unspoken emotions and the knowledge that the coming days would test them all in ways they had yet to imagine.

That night, Kelu couldn't sleep. He kept thinking about what would happen in the coming days. Lots to do, and the planning needed to be perfect.

If something went wrong, so many people's lives would be destroyed. He knew he was being selfish. He started thinking about Vinay. His friend could lose all his possessions, possibly even his life.

At one point, Kelu thought perhaps he should stop this craziness. Then, his mind went back to Lakshmi. Her beauty haunted him. The tender touch of her breast on his chest made him crazy. He wanted her at any cost. He fell asleep at some point.

It thrilled Vinay to think about how his life would change as of tomorrow. He looked at his wife, who was sleeping by him.

He was so happy with how she had supported him with these plans. He hugged her.

Savitri turned toward him and asked, 'What happened? Not sleeping?' He just smiled at her and kissed her.

She whispered, 'These days you are too much, you big romantic.'

Both giggled.

Early the following day, while the sun was still hiding, Vinay and Kelu went to Nanu's house.

From far away they could see the entire family waiting outside with a lantern.

Kelu put a hand on Vinay's shoulder and said, 'I cannot believe it is happening, my friend. I am the luckiest man today.'

Nanu said as they approached the family, 'Thampra, our lives are in your hands. Please do not play tricks on us. I am happy for Lakshmi, but I am worried about her siblings. We are surrendering everything to you. Take us and protect us, Thampra.'

Kelu realized it would be an enormous responsibility, and for a moment, it scared him. But he suddenly regained his confidence.

'Nanu, never have second thoughts. Once I set my mind on something, I always follow through. Now, take all the clothes we brought and get ready. Today onward you are not a Thattan family. You are a Nair family now, so behave like one.'

Kelu paused, gathering his thoughts, then continued with renewed determination. 'This change isn't just about a new identity. It's about claiming your place in society and ensuring a better future for our family. You have worked hard to get here, and you deserve every bit of success coming your way. Hold your head high, and don't let anyone make you feel less than you are. You have the strength and the courage to face any challenge.'

He looked at Nanu with a reassuring smile. 'Remember, our worth isn't determined by our past but by how we shape our future. So, let's step into this new chapter with confidence and pride.'

Kelu felt good after that speech and felt back in control. He needed to take charge and not let this family lose their confidence in him.

He knew Vinay and his family would play their parts well, but Nanu's family needed to learn a lot, and their confidence in him should be complete. Kelu had a separate bag for Lakshmi. He wanted her to be perfect when she dressed up.

Lakshmi stood behind her mom and did not look at him. He went closer. Her mom pushed her forward. He looked at her in the light from the lantern her mother was holding.

He could look at her for the first time without getting scared or worried about others. He held the bag out to her. She didn't move a finger.

Taking her hands and placing the bag in them, he asked her to dress quickly and come back out. She looked at him, and he saw tears in her eyes.

Lakshmi turned and walked toward her house. She knew there was no turning back here. Was this real? Would he actually do what he was saying? Her heart pounded hard. She was not at all convinced.

She turned back and looked at her mom. She saw happiness in everyone's eyes. They were all dreaming big. She prayed to God and continued inside.

Kelu was confused by her tears. Did she actually agree to this marriage, or was she doing this out of fear? He wanted to know.

He asked Nanu, 'Can I talk to Lakshmi for a minute before we go?'

'Thampra, she is yours. You can do whatever you want.'

Kelu grabbed Nanu by the neck and said, 'She is not a commodity here. She's a human being. I am not here to use her however I want. I am here to marry her. Never talk like this again. Do you understand?'

The fire in his eyes scared Nanu. He apologized as Vinay pulled Kelu away.

Kelu went into the house.

Lakshmi looked stunning in her new clothes and jewellery. Her beauty and elegance, along with the clothes, put her right where

Kelu wanted to portray her. No one would think she was from a low caste. Lakshmi stood still and never looked up to his face.

Kelu took her chin and tilted it up to look at him. She was shivering, and tears came rolling down her cheeks.

He looked at her and smiled. 'I am not here to hurt you or your family. I promise. I love you and want to take you as my wife. I assure you I will take care of you till I die. Please tell me you also want this.'

Lakshmi said nothing.

'Okay, if you don't say anything, I will go. I do not want to force someone to come and live with me. I will still fulfil my promise to my friend's family and yours. So, please travel with them to Pala. Have a pleasant life. I will not disturb you. Vinay will take care of your family as per our plans, regardless.'

Kelu turned to leave.

Lakshmi grabbed his hand and pulled him toward her. 'I am scared,' she said. 'I love my family. I want them to live with me till they get settled in their own lives. I am all yours, but please give me word that you will allow what I ask.'

'I promise. You don't worry, they are my family now, too.'

Kelu realized the sun was peeking out. 'Come on everyone we need to move,' he called out.

Vinay was ready with Kelu's bullock cart.

Kelu said, 'Take them to Pala. Make sure you cover the back of the cart. No one should see anyone until you get out of this town. I will bring Savitri and Kannan on another cart.'

Kelu watched Lakshmi climb into the cart.

She smiled at him. Kelu wanted to get into the cart with her, but he had to function now. He ran back to Vinay's house, where Savitri and Kannan stood outside with their belongings.

'What you took so long?' she yelled at him.

'Don't you want to get out of town before the sun rises? I almost fainted here thinking something had gone wrong.'

Kelu said nothing. He quickly readied the other cart and they set off to Pala without further delay.

Throughout the journey, no one talked. Everyone was lost in their own thoughts.

Nanu was concerned. He felt like he was selling his daughter.

He wanted to ask her whether she was happy but held his tongue. His wife was sleeping. She was like that and could easily fit into any situation.

Nanu felt the cart slowing down. He woke everyone up. 'We might be there,' he whispered. 'Do not talk to anyone. Just act as though we are rich. Vinay Thampra will speak for us. Don't forget.'

The cart started moving again, this time faster. He realized they had not reached Pala yet. His wife got mad at him. She'd been in deep sleep when he woke her. She shoved him, then lay down and rested her head on Lakshmi's lap.

Lakshmi smiled at her father, for the first time since they'd left the house. He realized his daughter was okay. He rested his head on the side of the cart carriage and closed his eyes.

Silence crept in as their bodies moved with the cart's rhythm.

Hours went by. Nanu woke as the cart came to a sudden halt. He could hear many people outside the cart. His heart raced.

He could see from Lakshmi's face that she was worried. He nudged his wife, and she woke up mad. Lakshmi smiled, and her siblings all tried not to laugh. A bright light came in as the back of the carriage opened.

It was Kelu. He smiled and reached his hand in for Lakshmi to step down.

Lakshmi looked at Nanu, who told her to go. She went out, and rest stayed in the carriage.

Vinay poked his head in and said, 'We have passed the dangerous part. Now we are in a different village. No one knows us here. From here on, we can travel without hiding. Lakshmi will travel with Kelu in the other cart.' He left the cover open.

Nanu looked back and saw Lakshmi sitting with Kelu. Lakshmi was talking and laughing.

Lakshmi's siblings giggled, and their mother told them to keep quiet. Nanu went back to sleep. His age was taking a toll on him, and travel tired him.

They travelled all day long. The sun slipped below the horizon and it was getting dark.

Kelu felt Lakshmi's hand near his hand. He held her hand. She looked inside the carriage and saw Savitri and Kannan were sleeping.

She smiled at Kelu and rested her head on his shoulder. Kelu felt like he was floating. He raised her hand and kissed it.

Lakshmi moved closer to him. Their bodies swayed with the rhythm of the cart.

'Why were you scared when I met you for the first time?' Kelu asked.

Lakshmi did not say anything for a while, and then she said, 'I am from low caste. I did not know how you were or what were your intentions. I needed to be very careful. I was terrified then, and I am still scared now. I am doing this for my family's benefit, but I am still worried in my heart. Please don't take this as an insult. I want to trust you. Please give me more time. You would understand my feelings if you knew what happened to one of my classmates.'

'Will you tell me what happened?'

Lakshmi looked outside the cart for a while. They moved through unlit roads. The lamp in the front of the cart was the only thing anyone could see.

Finally, she said, 'I am certain you know many stories like this. Still, I will tell you what happened. I did not sleep for many days after the incident, which happened to my best friend, Kanya. She was taller and more beautiful than me. One day, while coming back from our school, a guy from our village who hails from an upper-caste family asked her to go with him. She refused, and he got mad. He came back that night with many people and was surrounded by her house. They set it on fire.'

'She and her parents rushed out, crying. He grabbed her and tied her to his bullock cart. Then the crowd thrashed her parents in front of her. She cried out, asking him to leave her parents alone. We joined in, begging them to stop. But they did not. Her parents were thrashed until they lost consciousness, then they were stripped and hanged. Kanya was then brutally raped and, when they were done, thrown onto the street. No one dared to help her.

The image of her face covered in blood haunts me. Later that week, she killed herself.'

Lakshmi turned and looked at Kelu. 'See, I am same as Kanya. Now you tell me, should I be happy when you approached me? How can you men do such cruelty to us?'

Kelu could see the fire in her eyes. He realized how traumatized she was by the incident. He said nothing. Lakshmi sobbed for a while then, exhausted, she fell asleep.

Kelu watched Lakshmi's face glowing in the grace of moonlight as he directed the cart through the night.

Toward midnight, they reached Pala.

Kelu and Vinay stepped down from their carts while everyone else stayed.

Tension mounted when Kelu and Vinay did not immediately return. Everyone was quiet, only the bullocks making noise.

Kelu came running back. 'Okay, everyone, we have the key for the house. Take all your belongings and follow me.'

Lakshmi jumped out of the cart and Kelu smiled at her. They walked together in front, and the rest followed. No one talked.

They were all hungry and tired. Kannan was still sleeping on Savitri's shoulder.

Nanu carried almost everybody's luggage on his shoulders and head. He struggled a bit.

Vinay saw them coming and came running to take some luggage from Nanu. He got upset with Kelu. 'Don't forget, he's your beloved's father. Treat him with some respect. At least think about his age.'

They unlocked the door to the house Kelu had arranged, and the creaking wooden door gave way to a spacious interior.

As they stepped inside, Lakshmi's breath caught in her throat. The house was far more than just 'big enough'—it was magnificent by her standards.

The tall, intricately carved wooden columns held up high ceilings adorned with ornate beams. Sunlight filtered through large, arched windows, casting warm patterns on the polished stone floor.

Each room seemed to flow seamlessly into the next, with wide doorways and ample space, creating a sense of freedom she had never experienced before.

Lakshmi couldn't help but notice the attention to detail. The walls were decorated with hand-painted murals, and the furniture, though minimal, was elegant and refined, made of rich teak with smooth, flowing curves.

Soft rugs lay on the floor, their intricate patterns weaving tales of distant lands. Even the lamps, with their delicate metalwork, emitted a gentle glow that made the place feel warm and welcoming.

As Lakshmi wandered from room to room, her awe grew with every step. This was a world away from the cramped, mud-walled hut she had called home.

She could hardly believe that this was the place Kelu had chosen for them—a place so grand, so tasteful, and so far beyond what she could have ever imagined.

The spacious courtyard, the sturdy wooden doors, and the overall craftsmanship of the house spoke volumes about Kelu's wealth and his discerning eye for quality. Lakshmi felt a surge of gratitude, mixed with disbelief. This house wasn't just a shelter; it was a dream she had never dared to dream.

She realized how fortunate she was, not just because of Kelu's wealth but because he had put so much thought into where she and her family would live.

As she stood in one of the rooms, running her fingers along the smooth surface of a finely crafted wooden chest, she heard Kelu's voice echo through the house.

He was calling everyone to gather in the hall. Lakshmi quickly made her way to the central room, where she found the others already seated on comfortable cushions placed in a semi-circle.

Kelu stood in the centre of the hall, his face serious but calm. 'Please, everyone, sit,' he said, gesturing for Lakshmi to join them.

She took a seat, still absorbing the overwhelming emotions stirred by this unexpected new life. As she settled in, Lakshmi couldn't shake the feeling that she was incredibly lucky—lucky to have found someone who not only cared for her but also had the means to offer her and her family a better life, far beyond anything they had ever known.

'Tomorrow is a big day. For the first time, this town will see you all. Make sure you all play your parts well. Give them nothing to suspect. If we do, then we will have to start over in another town. Do not call me Thampra anymore. Don't show over respect. You are no longer low caste. I have bribed people to get new identities for everyone. Nanu, they will know you as Krishnan and your wife is Rama. Lakshmi, you stay as it is.'

He gave the other three siblings their new identities.

The next morning, Kelu asked everyone to get ready for the shop's grand opening.

They practiced with each other how they should portray themselves outside. The way they should walk and speak, and their names. Everything was different.

Kelu looked at them and shook his head. He got worried every time they slipped back into their slang. He advised them to talk as little as possible until they were comfortable.

After they finished their morning meal, they made their way to the shop—a modest but well-constructed building located at the heart of the bustling market.

As they approached, Lakshmi noticed the intricate wooden carvings on the shop's entrance, a detail that gave the place a touch of elegance despite its humble size.

The signboard above the door, painted with traditional motifs, announced the name of the shop in flowing Malayalam script.

A garment store, filled with handwoven textiles, vibrant silks, and cotton fabrics neatly displayed on wooden shelves lining the walls.

The shop was already buzzing with activity when they arrived. Word had spread quickly, and a crowd had gathered to see the new establishment.

Inside, the air was thick with the rich scent of freshly dyed cloth and sandalwood incense. Lamps hung from the ceiling, casting a warm glow on the neatly folded stacks of saris, dhotis, and veshtis.

Customers moved about, admiring the vibrant colours and fine textures, while Vinay and the workers attended to them, offering samples and explaining the quality of the fabrics.

The shop's interior was simple but functional—wooden counters, earthen jars holding dyes, and shelves filled with carefully organized garments. Each detail spoke of the care that had gone into setting up the business.

As the activity grew, Kelu stood quietly in a corner, his eyes closed in silent prayer. He knew how crucial this first day was for Vinay and his family, and he left nothing to chance.

He prayed for good fortune, steady customers, and a prosperous future for the shop. His hands tightened around the prayer beads in his palm as he whispered his hopes under his breath.

Meanwhile, Lakshmi played her role perfectly. She moved gracefully through the shop, greeting customers with a warm smile and assisting them with their selections.

She spoke with a natural ease, offering suggestions and making everyone feel welcome. Her calm demeanour and the way she handled even the smallest details impressed Kelu.

He watched her from a distance, pride swelling in his chest. In that moment, he knew he had chosen the right partner—a woman who could carry herself with grace and contribute to the success of this endeavour.

By the end of the day, the shop had done well—far better than anyone had anticipated. The shelves were noticeably emptier, and the jingle of coins in the cashbox was a testament to the day's success.

Vinay couldn't hide his gratitude. 'Kelu, I can't thank you enough,' he said, his voice thick with emotion. 'You've set everything up for us. We wouldn't have had such a start without you.' He reached into the cashbox, pulling out a handful of coins. 'Please, take the profit. It's only fair after everything you've done.'

But Kelu shook his head firmly. 'I gave my word to your wife, Vinay. This is your business now, not mine. You've worked hard and deserve every bit of it. Keep the profit and make sure you take care of this shop and your family.'

His voice was steady, but there was an underlying warmth in it. 'I'll be returning home today, as planned. After three months, you'll come to our town as we discussed. Until then, this is in your hands.'

Vinay's eyes glistened with gratitude as he nodded, understanding the significance of Kelu's gesture. Kelu's refusal to take any profit was not just an act of generosity; it was a sign of trust and respect.

Lakshmi, standing beside him, felt a deep admiration for Kelu. His selflessness and commitment to his word only confirmed the faith she had placed in him.

The bustling market outside began to quiet as dusk fell, and the flickering lamps inside the shop cast long shadows on the walls, marking the end of a successful first day.

As they prepared to close the shop, Kelu took one last look at the place, feeling a sense of fulfilment. Everything had gone according to plan, and now it was time to move on to the next step of their journey.

Kelu left. He did not even say goodbye to Lakshmi, he was so focused on the next steps.

Lakshmi was confused and asked Vinay why Kelu had not said goodbye to her.

Vinay said, 'Don't worry, Lakshmi. He's in a hurry to marry you. That's why. He's swimming against the current these days. I know him very well, and he is madly in love with you. Look at all of this. He created this world just so he could marry you. He's a kind man. You will not regret it.'

As the months passed, Nanu's family transformed into Krishnan's family. He became Vinay's right hand in all aspects of business.

In the meantime, Kelu kept talking to his friends and neighbours about Vinay's business and his partners. Kelu made sure the story about their success flourished in his hometown.

When Vinay thought they were ready, he and Savitri took Krishnan, Rama, Lakshmi and her siblings to Kelu's hometown. Everyone they passed talked about Lakshmi's beauty.

Kelu advised Vinay to take her around the town. They made a special trip to the temple.

Lakshmi had never entered a temple until that day, and she shivered with fear.

She told Vinay, 'I have never entered one before. I do not know what to do inside the temple.'

Vinay realized his fault right away. He should have taken her to a temple prior to coming here. He sent his cart back to fetch Savitri. While they waited outside, a lot of people walked by them.

Everyone looked at Lakshmi. Some even stumbled on the steps as they kept looking at her. Lakshmi giggled.

Vinay saw a familiar face coming from the temple. She walked toward them and Vinay's heart raced. Did she know Lakshmi from somewhere? When she got closer, he realized it was Kelu's mom.

Vinay smiled and introduced Lakshmi to her.

Kelu's mom moved closer to Lakshmi and held her chin. 'Girl, you look like a goddess. Watch out for the eagles around here.' She then turned and asked Vinay, 'Why are you standing here?'

'Savitri is on her way. We will go inside the temple together.'

A cart arrived and Savitri exited quickly.

Vinay gave her a reassuring look. She smiled and walked toward them.

Vinay reintroduced Savitri to Kelu's mom. They knew each other but had not seen each other for a very long time.

Kelu's mom said, 'Savitri, you really have become a woman of dreams. Vinay must be very lucky. I don't know when Kelu will get married. I wish he could find someone soon. Vinay, tell Kelu to get settled. I am getting old. I cannot take care of his house anymore.' She looked at Lakshmi and sighed.

Vinay and Lakshmi could already sense the unspoken wish in Kelu's mother's eyes—her desire to have Lakshmi as her daughter-in-law.

As she turned to leave, her voice took on a commanding tone. 'Vinay, make sure you speak to Kelu. And before you go, I expect all of you at our home for dinner. Tomorrow.'

Vinay, with a respectful nod, replied, 'It would be an honour, madam. We will certainly be there.'

Back at Kelu's house, the evening breeze gently stirred the coconut palms as his mother called him to the dining area, where she was seated on a low wooden bench by the brass oil lamp.

Kelu stood by the carved teak pillar, his gaze focused on the flickering flame. His mother's sharp eyes caught his distracted demeanour.

'Kelu, have you seen Vinay and his family since they arrived?' she asked, her voice carrying a hint of impatience.

'Yes, Mother. I've met them. They've been here for a few days now,' Kelu replied, shifting slightly but still avoiding her gaze.

His mother's face tightened with disappointment. 'And you never thought to tell me? He was your closest friend! After all these years, he's back, and you couldn't even invite them to our home? I had to meet them at the temple and invite them myself.'

Kelu straightened, sensing the weight of her words. This was not merely a casual dinner; it was the first step in a carefully orchestrated plan.

'I'll extend the invitation, Mother. When do you want them to come?'

'Tomorrow evening. All of them. You must be here too. Nothing else matters more right now.' Her tone left no room for argument.

Without delay, Kelu set off to meet Vinay. The path wound through familiar groves, the air heavy with the scent of jasmine and damp earth.

As he approached Vinay's temporary lodging, memories of their youthful days together flashed in his mind. The small cottage where they stayed was nestled between thick groves of plantains.

Kelu paused, adjusting his shawl, trying to clear his mind of the uneasy thoughts of what lay ahead. He knocked on the door, the sound echoing in the quiet evening.

Vinay himself answered the door, his expression turning from surprise to warmth as he recognized his old friend.

Lakshmi was behind him, her eyes lighting up at the sight of Kelu.

Kelu wasted no time, but his tone was laced with careful urgency.

'Vinay, the day we've been preparing for has finally arrived. Tomorrow is crucial. My mother has invited all of you to dinner. Remember, no exaggerations—just be natural. We can't afford any slip-ups. My mother isn't easily fooled.'

Vinay exchanged a knowing glance with Lakshmi before responding, 'We understand, Kelu. We'll be there, and we'll stick to the plan. This has to work out smoothly.'

Kelu nodded, satisfied but tense. As he turned to leave, his gaze softened when it met Lakshmi's. He hadn't seen her up close in a long while, and for a moment, everything else faded.

The lamplight played gently across her delicate features, casting shadows that accentuated her grace. Her long hair, loosely braided, swayed as she moved, and her eyes held a depth that drew him in.

'You will be mine, Lakshmi,' he whispered, his voice barely audible, yet full of conviction. 'I promise.'

Lakshmi met his gaze, her eyes holding a mix of emotions—uncertainty, hope, and a quiet resolve.

Kelu's heart raced as he took in every detail of her presence, as if capturing a moment, he could revisit again and again.

He could sense that the game was shifting, and tomorrow would be a turning point for all of them.

Krishnan left the room to give them some privacy. Savitri pulled Vinay out of the room as well. Lakshmi's siblings ran away giggling.

Kelu held Lakshmi's shoulder and nuzzled her. She just looked down to the floor.

He pulled her chin up and smiled at her. 'I missed you a lot. I don't know how I lived this long doing nothing but stupidity. If it was not for you, I would have turned this world upside down. You taught me a lot of patience.'

They both laughed. He hugged her, and they stood there for a while, lost in the moment.

Vinay finally came back and said, 'Kelu, it's time to leave. I don't want you to be in my house for too long. We need to play this safe.'

He pushed Kelu out the door.

Lakshmi sat quietly on the verandah, her gaze drifting across the sprawling courtyard bathed in the soft glow of the setting sun.

The once-familiar landscape now felt like a distant memory, as if she were living in someone else's world. Only a few months ago, she was trapped in a life of poverty and despair.

Her family barely managed to have one full meal a day, let alone three. Her clothes were threadbare, and the prospect of a better future seemed impossible.

Yet here she was, preparing to marry into the wealthiest family in the village, a twist of fate that still left her in disbelief.

She turned her attention to the small wooden mandir placed in a corner of the verandah, where an image of Lord Krishna hung on the wall, adorned with fresh jasmine garlands and glowing softly in the light of an oil lamp.

The dark, mischievous eyes of the deity seemed to watch her; his flute poised in eternal melody. For a moment, Lakshmi's expression hardened as memories flooded back.

She had never been one to pray or seek divine help; in fact, she had resented Lord Krishna and the gods for as long as she could remember.

To her, the gods were indifferent, watching from their distant heavens as the caste system dictated the lives and fates of people like her. Lakshmi's family, being of low caste, had suffered immensely under the rigid social order.

They were treated as less than human by those of higher caste—insults, abuse, and indignity had been part of their daily lives. She often wondered how a god like Krishna, revered by so many, could stand by and let such injustice persist.

But now, sitting in this grand home, on the brink of a new life, Lakshmi couldn't shake the feeling that perhaps it wasn't Krishna's divine plan, but sheer luck, that had brought her here.

Yet even as she acknowledged her fortune, she was not naive. The system that oppressed people like her still thrived, and Lakshmi knew that her own elevation in status would do nothing to change that.

However, she had made up her mind—she would not allow herself to become complacent or disconnected from her roots. She had a new purpose now.

Her thoughts turned to the many low-caste women who were still suffering—women like her who faced daily humiliation and the constant threat of violence.

Lakshmi's eyes blazed with determination as she silently vowed to use her newfound position to help them.

She would find ways to uplift these women, to help them stand on their own two feet, to protect them from those who would prey on them.

Most of all, she would fight back against the horrific practice of raping low-caste women, a crime that was often ignored or even justified by those in power.

With these thoughts solidifying in her heart, Lakshmi turned back to the picture of Lord Krishna. For the first time, she felt a sense of resolve in her relationship with the deity.

'Krishna,' she whispered, her voice steady but filled with quiet defiance, 'if you truly are the protector of the weak, you better stand with me in this fight. I don't need your blessings if it means allowing injustice to continue. But if you're with me, we will change this together.'

The flame in the lamp flickered, casting long shadows that danced across the walls, and Lakshmi felt an unexpected calm wash over her.

This was the beginning of her journey—not just as a bride-to-be in a wealthy household, but as a warrior for those who had no voice.

With Krishna's picture watching over her, she knew her resolve was unshakable. She said one more time, this time with a louder voice and more conviction: - 'Krishna, you better be with me!!!

As she said that, her father came in. 'I heard. You may get married to a king, but I am still your father. Don't forget that.' He walked away.

Lakshmi had no clue, why he'd reacted that way. Then she realized he must have thought she was talking to him. She giggled to herself.

She also remembered a story she'd heard about the Udupi temple. People had started to flock there, as they'd heard an Idol of Krishna turn in the direction of a low-caste devotee.

Is this going to be a change for us? she wondered. Even God was showing us signs. Oh, Lord, please show us some mercy. We have suffered enough. I have seen enough already. Many of my friends have already perished, and families are still suffering.

The following evening, as dusk painted the skies in hues of purple and gold, Kelu's house was buzzing with anticipation.

The courtyard was adorned with oil lamps placed along the pathways, their soft glow welcoming the guests. The fragrance of incense mingled with the scent of jasmine garlands draped along the entrance.

Kelu stood near the doorway, adjusting the pleats of his dhoti, his eyes constantly flitting towards his mother. She was a woman of sharp instincts and rarely missed a detail. Tonight, he needed everything to go smoothly.

As Vinay and his family arrived, the air crackled with a mix of excitement and apprehension.

Vinay wore a simple yet dignified attire—his freshly pressed dhoti paired with a clean white shirt that showed his modest upbringing, while Lakshmi looked every bit the traditional bride-to-be.

She was draped in a beautiful silk sari, its deep green contrasting with the gold zari work, while her braided hair was adorned with fresh flowers.

Her eyes, lined with kajal, held a quiet resolve. Kelu noticed his mother's gaze lingering on Lakshmi, even as she warmly greeted Vinay and the others.

The subtle smile on his mother's lips hinted that she liked what she saw, but Kelu couldn't shake off his worry. If anyone could sense something was amiss, it would be her.

The initial greetings flowed smoothly, with everyone exchanging pleasantries. The women gathered in one corner, admiring Lakshmi's sari and jewellery, while the men discussed everything from harvests to local festivals.

Kelu's mother, ever the gracious host, ensured everyone was comfortable.

She had arranged for spiced tea and sweetened coconut water, which were served in brass tumblers by the household help.

Plates of banana chips, murukku, and other traditional snacks were passed around as people eased into conversation. The clinking of bangles, the rustle of silk, and the low hum of voices filled the room, creating an atmosphere that was lively yet laced with underlying tension.

Kelu watched as his mother moved with practiced grace among the guests, offering more snacks and making polite conversation.

Her eyes, though, always seemed to return to Lakshmi. It was a game of observation—an unspoken examination. Lakshmi, to her credit, remained poised, smiling demurely when spoken to, yet Kelu noticed a faint unease in her eyes whenever his mother's gaze lingered a little too long.

His chest tightened with anxiety. This was the moment he had been dreading. He had to tread carefully—one wrong move, one slip of the tongue, and his mother's sharp mind would catch on.

After everyone had mingled and relaxed, Kelu signalled subtly to Vinay. The plan was simple but delicate: steer the conversation towards the marriage proposal naturally, without raising suspicions.

The group gathered in the drawing room, a cozy space with intricately carved wooden furniture and cushions embroidered with traditional motifs.

The oil lamps flickered in the breeze, casting warm shadows across the room as everyone settled in. Kelu's mother took her seat on the main sofa, her sari neatly pleated, her expression unreadable. Kelu could feel her presence like a hawk in the room, watching, waiting.

Vinay cleared his throat lightly, exchanging a quick glance with Kelu before speaking. 'Aunty,' Vinay said, 'we are looking for a groom for Lakshmi. My partner, Krishnan, thinks Kelu is the right fit for her. What do you say?'

Lakshmi acted shocked. She looked at Vinay with a bit of anger on her face. Kelu really liked that move. He smiled at her.

Kelu's mother didn't respond immediately. She simply looked at Vinay, her eyes narrowing slightly as she considered his words. Her fingers absentmindedly traced the edge of her pallu, a habit Kelu recognized as her way of thinking things through.

The room seemed to grow quieter, the atmosphere shifting as everyone sensed that the conversation had taken a serious turn.

Kelu's heart raced, his mind racing with possibilities. Would she agree without questioning? Or would she probe deeper, uncovering what he and Vinay had so carefully hidden?

Lakshmi, sitting slightly apart from the others, could feel the weight of the moment. She clasped her hands together in her lap, her knuckles whitening as she braced herself for whatever might come next.

She knew she had to remain calm, to let Vinay and Kelu handle this, but the intensity in Kelu's mother's eyes made her uneasy.

After what felt like an eternity, Kelu's mother finally spoke.

She looked at Krishnan and said, 'Are you sure? You really don't know my son. He is not willing to marry anyone. I have proposed many alliances before. It seems like he will never marry. As a mother, I would love to get my son married and settled. I'd love Lakshmi as my daughter-in-law, but why don't you ask yourself? He's right here. If he says yes, I am all for it.'

Everyone looked at Kelu.

Kelu said, 'Well, everyone seems to be behind me getting married. Fine. If that is what you all want, I will do it. This is crazy.'

Krishnan knew Kelu was playing his part. He said to put oil on the fire, 'If that's the case, I don't want to force you. My daughter wants someone who is interested in having a family. Vinay, we will see whether it suits someone else nearby in your town to have her.'

Kelu stared at him. His mind raced. He hadn't expected that from Krishnan. 'I did not say I am getting forced. I said, I am ready.'

Everyone laughed except Kelu.

Kelu saw Lakshmi hiding her face and laughing, too. He didn't enjoy that a bit. He wanted to kill Krishnan. How dare he behave like that? Acting was good, but that could have derailed everything.

After a few hours, they all left.

On the way to the carts, Kelu grabbed Krishnan's hand and squeezed it hard. 'Don't you ever do that kind of clever talk again,' he warned. 'I will put you back where you belong.'

Krishnan winced from the pain as he apologized. Lakshmi saw the tension between them and came over. 'I will take care of this,' she said.

The way Kelu looked at her filled her eyes with tears.

'Don't cry,' he said. 'I cannot see that. Leave now.'

Days passed by. Everyone was in marriage preparation mode.

Kelu couldn't wait. He got a priest to allot a date as soon as possible. He wanted the marriage to be the best the village had ever seen.

He had the organizer put a grand tent in front of his house and made sure the entire village's streets leading to his house got lit.

He installed oil lamps everywhere. He used many people to make sure they stayed lit throughout the week.

People around the village raved about the decorations. He brought in many performers, who performed on various stages around the town.

He even invited the king to come in for the marriage. The gold ornaments he got were custom-made. Being a man who used to make gold ornaments himself, Krishnan had a lot of opinions and did not like many of the pieces. Kelu ignored him.

On the day of the wedding, villagers gathered outside the house to get a glimpse of this princess. They'd heard from many people she was like an apsaras—a dancer from heaven.

Kelu arranged a grand carriage for her, with four sturdy men to carry it. They led her in a procession with five elephants and many performers. She cried all the way in. She couldn't believe she was getting married in such lavish surroundings.

Kelu wanted to give her the best. He wanted her to feel like an actual princess. Many dancers performed in front of her as she watched from her carriage.

Then Kelu's mom came in front of her carriage. She was carrying an oil lamp, followed by a few others who carried plates with vermillion and lemon.

Villagers talked among themselves 'What is happening here? The groom's mother is welcoming the bride. Rich people do as they please these days.' The custom is the bride's family welcoming the groom.

Lakshmi stepped out of the carriage, and everyone gasped in wonder. She was in a red saree, adorned with gold ornaments from neck to naval.

She had a gold ornament on her hair, gold jewellery on her ears, and both hands up to the elbows. She looked at the villagers and smiled.

They all cheered and called her princess. She felt out of place, but tried to keep her composure.

The surrounding people pushed each other to try and see her.

Vinay directed his companions to control the crowd and help Lakshmi out. She walked toward Kelu's mother, who looked thrilled. Kelu's mother washed Lakshmi's feet. Villagers did not like that a bit. No one said anything.

She gave the oil lamp to Lakshmi and asked her to follow her to the tent. Upon entering the tent, she couldn't believe how beautifully it was decorated. She was speechless. Tears started to flow. Her mother tried to wipe her tears.

Lakshmi said, 'No, Mother. I am living my life now. Let me.' She walked around, looking at everything. Many drapes matched her saree.

Kelu had gone above and beyond. She was so proud of him. She saw Kelu sitting in the mandap where the marriage would happen.

They even decorated the mandap with large oil lamps, red materials, and lots of flowers from top to bottom. The place smelled like a garden.

She entered the mandap and Kelu couldn't stop looking at her. He could not believe this woman would be his wife soon.

She sat near him and smiled. Her beauty dumbfounded Kelu. He just sat there.

Suddenly, a prominent voice said, 'Kelu!' He got jolted. Everyone around laughed. It was Vinay, who had the mangalasutra ready for him.

Kelu took the mangalasutra and tied it around Lakshmi's neck. It was a beautiful necklace with black beads and gold.

Lakshmi looked at it and smiled at Kelu. He whispered, 'You are mine, and I am yours.'

He got up, and Lakshmi did the same.

They walked around the fire holding hands.

Kelu led her four times, and then Lakshmi led three times. That concluded the ceremony.

After the wedding, everyone ate a grand meal.

Kelu had arranged different chefs for each dish, handpicking each one. It was a perfect meal.

Everyone raved about the taste. They didn't want to get up from the seats. They wanted to eat more, but their stomachs eventually became too full to continue. At some point, they had to get up and leave.

Kelu was so proud of the accomplishment. He realized how much everyone around him had helped.

He went to Vinay and Savitri. 'I owe you my life for doing this for me. I am so happy and blessed at the same time. I am the luckiest to have a wonderful wife and friends.'

He hugged Vinay, then he hugged Savitri.

That was a first. No one ever hugs someone else's wife. Vinay said nothing. He realized it was out of happiness that Kelu had done that. Savitri got panicked and looked around.

Some were looking at them in astonishment. She looked at Kelu. He was clueless. He was so happy that he didn't know what to do with himself.

She pinched Vinay for not saying anything.

Kelu walked away as if nothing unusual had happened. Vinay looked the other way and also walked away.

Savitri had a shy smile on her face; she kind of liked that hug. She glanced at Lakshmi, and the look they exchanged had some spark. Savitri quickly looked away.

The evening's entertainment started. There were many games. One was to find the groom's ring in a pot of milk. Both the groom and bride had to search for the ring simultaneously.

Belief was, whoever found the ring would rule the family. They fought hard, but Lakshmi got the ring. She whispered to him, 'I have it, but I want you to have it.'

Kelu said, 'I am okay with it. I love you to rule me always.'

Lakshmi pushed the ring into his hand and pulled it out. People clapped. Kelu just sat there smiling. He realized that his wife would take care of him and love him a lot. He was overcome with joy.

***

Years passed. Lakshmi gave birth to a girl. They named her Narayani, which was Goddess Lakshmi's other name.

'This girl was part of you, Lakshmi,' Kelu said. 'So, this name is apt for her.'

Now three years old, Narayani filled Vilasam Bungalow with happiness.

Narayani was everywhere. She never cried or disobeyed.

Kelu's mom always said, 'I am sure she's taking after you, Lakshmi. Kelu was never like this. You are lucky that she's such a sweet girl.'

Narayani always ate well and slept well. Bringing her up was easy. Life was perfect.

Kelu's business thrived, and his name and fame travelled all over the province. Villagers respected him for his abilities.

Vinay was still in Pala, spreading his business to many other towns. Lakshmi's siblings helped him with the business. They all moved out to different towns and took care of the distinct branches. Krishnan became a father figure for Vinay.

Vinay's and Kelu's families always met during the festival of lights. They'd all bonded very well.

Lakshmi and Savitri became close, but Savitri always felt uncomfortable around Kelu. She couldn't forget that moment he'd hugged her, and every time she saw Lakshmi that awkwardness always surfaced.

Lakshmi, for her part, didn't seem to care about it. Narayani liked Kannan, and they always played even though Narayani was younger. Kannan kept her entertained every time they saw each other.

Vinay wanted Kelu to join with him and do business together, but Kelu always refused. 'This friendship, love, and relationship we have now would suffer. I don't want that. Money is always a devil. We are happy; let it be.'

Vinay was a cautious person. He worried. 'What if something happens to one of us? Who would take care of our family? I want my wife and Kannan looked after.'

'If something happens to me, won't you take care of my daughter and wife?' Kelu asked.

'No doubt. You know I will.'

'Then what's the issue? Why do we need to merge business? I will always be there for your family. Don't you worry,' Kelu replied.

Vinay realized Kelu was the brother he never had. He felt so relieved that he never brought up the topic again.

***

Part Two: Pala

The outbuilding's door creaked open and jolted Kelu out of his thoughts.

'Who is it?'

'Bhavani wanted me to give you some blankets. Here, go to sleep. I do not want you to get sicker than you are now. I have no time to take care of you.' Surya threw a blanket on him and closed the door again.

Kelu took a deep breath as he wrapped the blanket around his shoulders.

Life had changed so much in one day. He couldn't believe how quickly he'd gone from a business owner to a prisoner in his house. He looked outside the window.

Plants and flowers shone in the moonlight. The slow breeze made the branches dance. He smiled and, for a moment, forgot about his situation. It didn't last long; the breeze brought the smell of the firepit.

Kelu cried as his thoughts drifted again, trying to figure out where things went wrong.

***

Vinay travelled all across the southern country for business. Sometimes, he had to travel overnight, and often, he had to stay away for days. Kelu had told him many times not to travel alone and also to avoid overnight travels if possible.

He always brushed this off by saying, 'Nothing will happen. I am always careful. I know my way around and always avoid dangerous routes.'

One day, after a regular trip, Vinay travelled back home at night. He wanted to surprise Kannan for his birthday. He let the bullocks pull the cart at their own pace in the night. They knew the way, and he never really had to guide them.

Suddenly, he saw a woman running toward his cart. It was a woman from a low caste. She was crying, and he could see she was bleeding from her nose.

Her undergarment was ripped almost entirely off, and Vinay right away knew she had been attacked.

He told her to get into his cart.

The situation scared him, as this was unlike when he took Lakshmi in disguise. Here, anyone could see her as low caste.

Vinay urged the bullocks to pull the cart a little faster.

A few people came running toward the cart running. One yelled at him. 'Did you see a low-caste woman going by?'

Vinay said, 'Yes, she went into that bush there,' then hastily continued.

As he passed, one guy looked into the cart and saw her. The group chased them on foot.

Travel had already tired out the bullocks. They couldn't go faster. The mob caught up with the cart and pulled it to the side.

Vinay jumped out of the cart.

The men were in their twenties. Young blood.

Vinay tried to stop them from pulling her out of the cart, and when they wouldn't stop, Vinay tried to persuade them with some money. They were not interested. They pulled her into the bush.

Vinay grabbed one guy and hit him hard. The other three came back and attacked. Vinay tried to fight back, but he was outnumbered four to one.

He looked around for wood or something to help himself, but his attackers were ruthless. They hit and kicked him over and over, and then one pulled out a knife and stabbed him, calling him a traitor. They stabbed him a few times and dragged him into the bush.

Vinay watched helplessly as they tied her hands and legs around trees. Her legs were wide open, and she was suspended. One by one, they raped her repeatedly, all the while calling out to Vinay.

'You idiot! See you could have enjoyed. Instead, you wanted to be a saint. Disgrace to our society.'

One of them spit on Vinay's face. Another one came back with the sperm and pasted on his body.

Vinay was bleeding heavily, and the woman was not moving anymore. Either dead or unconscious. Still, the men continued attacking her. Biting her, pulling her breasts, laughing and dancing around her.

Finally, one said, 'Hey, he offered us money. Let's go check out his cart.'

They went to his cart and took his money and merchandise.

When they came back, and looked at him. They realized he was still alive. The lady was not moving or breathing.

One of them took a knife and stabbed the woman in the chest a few times. She made a few movements. But they left nothing much in her. No sound came from her.

Another guy picked up a big rock. He yelled, 'Scoundrel, now you die!' He smashed the rock into Vinay's head.

Vinay cried and pleaded for his life. He said his son was waiting for him at home. But they didn't listen. They kept bashing his head until there was no doubt Vinay was dead.

They pulled him back to the road and left him with the cart, placing the dead woman on top of him.

As day broke and people who walked by saw them lying naked, stories flew.

Soon, Krishnan came to hear about the dead people by the cart, and he rushed to the spot. He couldn't believe what he saw there.

Vinay's head was smashed in, his body all cut. No one wanted to touch the low-caste woman lying on top of him.

Krishnan pushed everyone aside and pulled her body off. He gagged when he saw her private parts had been mutilated.

'God,' he screamed, 'why did you create people like this? Didn't you see this? Why are you so silent?'

He put both bodies in his cart and covered them with a tarp.

Some people tried to stop him, saying, 'You are inviting trouble here. Leave her and take only your family member.'

Krishnan did not answer, only rode away.

***

Kelu was devastated by the news. He raged, smashing all kinds of things in the house. He even beat the guy who came to tell him the grave news.

He became furious and cried a lot loud. Vinay was his life, the reason Kelu was happy. He paced furiously, weeping the whole time.

Lakshmi had never seen him like this. Kelu always had a calm mind. Now, he could not control his emotions. He would sit for a while staring at the wall and then cry for a bit. Then, back to the pacing.

This continued all day. No one wanted to ask him anything. Lakshmi kept Narayani away from him. She knew how hard it was for him, knew his deep connection with his beloved friend.

In the afternoon, Kelu started packing clothes. He knew he had to keep his promise to help Savitri and Kannan.

He looked at Lakshmi and said, 'I am leaving. I have to go to Pala.'

Lakshmi did not reply, but she helped him continue packing.

'Can you manage here? I will not be back for a while.'

Lakshmi was quiet as she left the room, but she came back with food for him to take on the journey. She saw Kelu sitting and crying.

She approached him, lifted his face, and said, 'My dear, I know your loss is tremendous. I can manage here. You should help his family. I will let you know if I need any help or have any difficulties. Just remember, you will be a father again in a few months. I will need you then for sure. Now, however, they need you more than me. I don't know how Kannan and Savitri are holding up,'

Kelu hugged her. He felt so relieved. His wife was understanding and mature. Most women would have stopped him from leaving, especially since she was being pregnant and had a younger daughter to take care of.

He felt so proud of his wife. He kissed her lips.

Lakshmi pushed him away. 'Someone will walk in, and it is dazzling and sunny.'

They both giggled.

Kelu called Narayani to him. 'Nanu, I am going to Pala. I will see Kannan, your friend. Do you want me to say anything?'

'First, stop calling me Nanu. Second, tell Kannan to stay away from me.' With a lot of attitude, she walked away.

Kelu and Lakshmi shook their heads and laughed.

Kelu talked to his workers and planned for business. He instructed them all to report to Lakshmi daily. He checked his cart and brought his favourite bullocks outside. His determination showed.

Lakshmi could see something was brewing. She watched him place a machete and an axe in the cart. Was he planning to get revenge? Lakshmi got worried. She went outside and approached him. She took his hands and put them on her full belly.

She said, 'I am not here to stop you, but if you are up to no good remember that you are a father and we are also important to you.' She did not say anything further and walked back inside.

Kelu realized his behaviour worried Lakshmi. He felt embarrassed. He sat down on the ground for a while and cried again, this time more from frustration.

Narayani came out and called to him. 'Appa, are you hurt? I can get you medicine.'

Kelu waved her off. He got up and prepared his cart ready for travel. As he finished packing his belongings, he saw the axe and machete in the cart. He thought about taking them out. Still, he left them in there. Just in case.

He looked around and called one of his workers over, and said something in his ear. The worker ran off to the field.

Lakshmi watched from the window. She knew Kelu would not listen to her. She could only pray.

They'd killed his closest ally, his best friend. It was not fair for her to stop him.

She knew Kelu was not stupid. He would make his move when it was right. Lakshmi knew that much.

She went to her prayer room. She prayed and brought out an oil lamp on a plate known as thali. Usually, a thali has an oil lamp, red vermilion, and a sacred thread. In this thali, she had a dagger.

She went out to the yard with Narayani. This time, her face was determined. Kelu saw her coming and he went to her.

Lakshmi instructed Narayani to do the religious ritual. Narayani took the oil lamp and went around her father's head three times.

Kelu stood with folded hands. He used his palm and took the blessings from the lamp's flame.

Lakshmi put vermilion on his forehead, then took the dagger out, cut her thumb, and placed the blood on his chest.

'Dear, go do what you have to do. If you have to take revenge, do it. My prayers are there for you. Those animals should not live. Do justice for your Vinay brother. I will take care of everything here.'

Kelu had never seen Lakshmi like this before. He took the dagger and placed it on his hip.

He lifted Narayani up and said, 'Take care of your mother. I will be back in a few days.'

Lakshmi corrected that. 'I will see you in a few months. I want you to go there and fix everything for them. Their business. Teach Kannan how to stand on his feet. Only then are you to come back. I can manage here.'

Lakshmi knew the importance of Kelu getting closure. Otherwise, she would see him suffering whenever there was some problem in Pala. She wanted to do the right thing, and saving her husband from misery was her priority.

The worker returned with a sack. One could see it was heavy.

Lakshmi frowned, wondering what it could be. She turned and went back in, determined to find out afterward what the worker had brought.

Kelu lifted the sack and put it into his cart. He gave the money to the worker and said, 'Don't you ever say anything about this to anyone. Not even to my wife. You say it was jackfruit for Kannan. She knows he loves it.'

Kelu ate some food and readied to set off late afternoon. Most of his travel would be after sunset, which was easier for the bullocks. He gave water and food to the bulls and tied them to the cart.

He was all set. This time, his travel was different. He had many plans. He usually took the easiest route, but this time he had some other things to do before he got to Pala.

He diverted his path and started traveling the same path Vinay had travelled. He wanted to see the location where he'd been killed.

After five hours, he reached the area. He could still see bloodstains on the ground. He walked inside the bush and saw the trees where the murders had occurred. He sat down and cried.

He'd been told that Vinay's skull had been broken in several places and that his face was not recognizable. Someone had used a heavy rock.

He returned to his cart and opened the bag his worker had prepared. Inside was a large rock. Kelu wanted to make sure he was prepared when he took revenge on those scoundrels. He didn't want to waste time looking for a rock.

Kelu entered the small toddy shop, his eyes sweeping over the dim, smoky interior. The hut was cramped, barely room for fifteen people.

The low hum of conversation died down as the men inside turned to look at him. In a town this small, strangers weren't common.

He was used to moving through places without stopping, but tonight was different. Tonight, he had business here.

He took in the narrow tables, the worn stools, and the shopkeeper wiping down the counter.

Kelu walked up and, without hesitation, ordered drinks for everyone. He needed to make a good impression. Then he turned to the crowd with a grin that didn't quite reach his eyes.

'Let's celebrate,' he said, his voice carrying just the right edge of casual malice.

'I heard someone here killed a man—some fool who tried to help a low-caste. He got what he deserved, didn't he? How dare he.'

The room erupted in cheers.

Kelu's pulse quickened. He was getting closer. Somewhere in this room were the men who knew what happened to Vinay, his closest friend. He needed to play this right.

A man stepped forward, his eyes gleaming as he approached Kelu. He looked about twenty-five, his build lean but muscular under the loose, sweat-stained tunic he wore.

His long, unkempt hair framed a face hardened by life, a thin scar slashing across his left cheek. He was a labourer, someone used to getting his hands dirty. His smile, however, was far too comfortable.

'Yeah, he deserved it,' the man said, and his voice dripping with pride. 'I was there. That woman? She's from here. I asked her plenty of times to come with me, but she refused. Should've known better. I could've kept her in my farmhouse with the others. I've got plenty of women there—they all do what I say. But this one… she didn't listen. So, I sent her up with that fool who wanted to be a saint.'

The man's laughter was loud, drawing his friends closer. He grabbed a tray of drinks and strutted over to a table where three others were sitting, all looking pleased with themselves.

Kelu's jaw clenched, but he kept his face neutral, watching them closely. This was it—these were the men. He was outnumbered and outmatched if he acted now. But the rage simmered beneath the surface, threatening to break his careful mask.

He moved across the room, slow and deliberate, his heart pounding as he approached the group.

'Hey,' Kelu said, flashing a grin, 'you've got a farmhouse and some low-caste women there, huh? See, it's been a while since I've had a proper good time. Think you could arrange something for tonight? I don't mind paying a little extra.'

The man turned to him, sizing him up. Kelu could feel the tension thickening in the air. The room, the drinks, the casual celebration—it was all a façade.

His real mission was finding out exactly what happened to Vinay. And to do that, he had to keep playing the game.

The guy gave Kelu a playful shove. 'Man, you are my friend now. You don't pay. I'll take you there and you chose who you want and that's it. In fact, we all are going there tonight. We are celebrating.'

Kelu said he would meet them outside and went back to his cart. He made sure the rock, machete, and axe were there for easy access. His determination overcame his fear. He wanted to do this for his friend. And that woman who died was around Lakshmi's sister's age. How could they do it? He sat and waited in the cart.

When the men staggered out of the toddy shop, their laughter loud and unrestrained, it was clear the alcohol had hit them hard.

Kelu, too, played the part—his steps unsteady, his grin loose, as if the drinks had dulled his senses. The men called out to him, telling him to follow, and he did, keeping pace as they stumbled along the narrow dirt road.

The journey took over half an hour, the night swallowing them as they left the village behind. The moon was hidden behind clouds, but far ahead, Kelu could make out a flicker of light—oil lamps glowed faintly in the distance, guiding their way.

As they approached, the scene became clearer. A large house stood on a slight rise, its walls illuminated by rows of oil lamps both outside and along the street leading up to it.

Kelu's sharp eyes didn't miss the subtle signs—this wasn't just any farmhouse. Whoever lived here had wealth, influence. But who was he?

Kelu parked the cart near the bushes, letting the bullocks graze and rest. He gave them water, his mind calculating.

The men had already gone ahead, disappearing into the house, their voices echoing in the night. Kelu washed his face and feet, wiping away the dirt of the road, and followed them inside.

The moment he crossed the threshold, Kelu felt the shift in the air. The house was immaculate, each corner spotless, each piece of furniture carefully placed.

The smell of incense filled his nose, mingling with the faint scent of sandalwood. He stepped into an enormous hall, the centrepiece of the house, with high ceilings and walls painted in muted tones.

The hall was circular, a strange design that made Kelu uneasy. There were doors leading off in every direction, each one likely leading to separate rooms, but there was only one way out—through the entrance he had just come through.

Kelu took it all in, his gaze sweeping the space as he moved further into the room. In the middle of the hall were several plush couches arranged in a circle. The men he had followed were lounging on them, still laughing loudly.

One of them, a broad-shouldered man with a patchy beard, was sprawled across a couch, his shirt open to reveal a thick gold chain around his neck.

Another, younger but equally muscular, had short-cropped hair and a jagged scar running down his forearm. He leaned back, resting his legs on the table in front of him.

A third man, shorter but stocky, sat on the edge of his seat, nervously picking at the dirt under his nails. His eyes darted around the room, as if he was always on edge, even among friends.

Kelu eased himself onto one of the couches, playing along, his posture relaxed but his senses sharp.

The men exchanged glances, still riding the high of their drunken bravado. They had no idea who they had brought into their den.

'Friend, you didn't come here to sit. Come. Let us show you the priceless commodities here.'

Kelu was disgusted by the use of that word, but he smiled and got up. He followed them to the fourth door on the left, which opened into a hallway lit by oil lamps.

The hallway led to another grand room, this time with the theme of a dance hall. There were many women there, all low caste.

They were laughing when the men walked in, but as soon as they saw the men, their happiness faded, and they stood in silence.

Kelu looked at them. They all were in their mid-twenties. He was so surprised to see so many of them at once.

The man whose house it was said, 'Choose any, friend. You can have up to three. More than that, you may not handle.'

They all laughed.

Kelu chose only one, the oldest of them. The guys joked with him. 'Why, the old lady? Come on, man, take this one. She came only yesterday.'

Kelu said nothing initially, then said, 'Okay, I will take her as well.' He realized if he didn't, she would probably get tortured by them tonight.

The older woman led Kelu into a room that hit him with a pungent, acrid smell. It was bare, almost suffocating so.

A simple cot sat in the centre, the thin mattress sagging from years of wear. There were no windows, only two dim oil lamps that flickered weakly, casting long shadows on the cracked walls. The air was heavy with the smell of sweat, old blood, and despair.

Kelu sat on the cot, his mind racing.

The older woman stood near the door, her posture firm and eyes hard, devoid of fear. She was in her mid-fifties, her skin weathered and marked with the signs of a difficult life.

Her grey hair was tied into a tight bun, and her sharp features carried the weight of too many unspeakable experiences.

There was a coldness about her, as though she had long accepted the life of servitude, but a trace of defiance flickered in her gaze.

Beside her, the girl was trembling, her body rigid with fear. She couldn't have been older than sixteen. Her wide, terrified eyes darted between Kelu and the older woman, her thin frame covered only by a frayed piece of cloth wrapped around her hips.

The girl's skin was marred with faint bruises, and her lips quivered as if she expected violence at any moment.

Her innocence was stripped away, replaced by the raw terror of what had already happened to her, and what she feared would happen next.

Kelu's heart clenched. He motioned for the woman to close the door. She obeyed without a word, turning slowly as if nothing in this world could faze her anymore.

With a swift, practiced motion, she reached over and pulled the cloth from the girl's body, stripping her of the last shred of dignity she had left.

The girl stood frozen, her eyes wide in shock, her breath coming in quick gasps.

'Hey, you. Stop,' Kelu said, his voice low but firm. 'Put that cloth back. Right now.'

The older woman didn't argue. She silently picked up the cloth and draped it back over the girl's hips, her face impassive, as if this was just another task in her daily routine.

Kelu leaned back, staring at the floor for a few moments, deep in thought.

The two of them stood by the door, their figures bathed in the flickering light of the oil lamps. The girl's terror hadn't lessened, and she clung to the doorframe as if it might save her.

The woman, on the other hand, stood stiffly beside her, her arms folded, her eyes cold and calculating.

Kelu raised his eyes to meet theirs. 'Would you like to escape?'

The words hung in the air for a second before the girl's eyes lit up with desperate hope. She stepped forward, her voice barely a whisper but filled with yearning. 'Yes, Thampra. Yes, please.'

But before she could say more, the older woman pinched her arm sharply, silencing her.

The girl recoiled, wincing, while the woman shot her a stern look—a warning. Her cautious gaze turned to Kelu, suspicion etched across her face.

Kelu got up and moved toward them slowly, trying not to startle the girl.

The older woman's protective instincts kicked in immediately. She placed herself between Kelu and the girl, her eyes narrowing as she pulled the trembling girl behind her.

'Sister,' Kelu said softly, his tone gentle, 'I am your friend. I want to help you.'

The woman didn't move. Her face remained stony, though there was a flicker of something behind her eyes—worn exhaustion, but also a mother's instinct to protect, even if the battle seemed already lost.

'My brother was killed by those men out there,' Kelu continued, his voice steady. 'They murdered him, just like they've hurt so many others. I want revenge, but I can't do it alone. Will you help me?'

The woman's face softened slightly, but she remained silent.

She had seen too much, suffered too long to trust easily. Her body bore the marks of years of abuse—deep scars, some visible, others hidden.

She had been beaten, starved, degraded. Those men outside had taken everything from her—her dignity, her freedom, her children. Her youngest daughter had been sold off years ago, and she had heard nothing since.

The girl by her side now, her niece, had been spared the worst of it so far, but only because the older woman had learned how to keep them both invisible.

Tears welled up in her eyes as she stood there, trembling. They weren't the kind of tears that came from fear—they were the tears of someone who had suffered silently for too long, who had kept her rage bottled up because it had nowhere to go.

After a long, agonizing moment, the woman finally spoke, her voice low and trembling with emotion.

'I have endured more than you can imagine, Thampra. Those men have taken everything from me.'

Her face hardened again, but this time, there was something new in her eyes. A fire. A spark of long-buried resistance.

'I would do anything to kill those bastards. Anything.'

Kelu nodded. He could see it now—the fierce determination in her. She wasn't broken. Not yet. And with her help, he might just have a chance at justice.

'I want you to show me the rooms where they are sleeping tonight. I chose you because I felt you are the leader for these girls. Was that correct?'

She nodded.

'Okay then. You go out now and leave this girl here. Tell the girls out there to make sure those guys get drunk tonight. If this goes as planned, I promise you everyone here will be free tonight. I will also take you to my home and you both can stay there helping my wife.'

They couldn't believe this was happening. They sat down and cried together a bit.

After a moment, Kelu said, 'Come now, we need to move.'

The woman got up and opened the door. She peeped her head outside, but no one was around. She went to the dance hall and cautiously looked around.

She wanted to choose the right girls for this job. Not everyone should know about it. She walked over to the one near the bar and asked her to follow.

They slipped into a room off the hallway, and after a few minutes, they came back out.

The woman went to the bar, grabbed a jug of drink and walked back to Kelu's room.

The guys noticed her outside, but they smiled when she showed them the drink jug. One yelled, 'Make sure you keep my friend happy. I don't want any complaints tomorrow.'

She turned and said, 'Thampra, don't you worry. Your friend will plead to stay.'

Everyone laughed.

She turned and continued; her face tight with anger. Her eyes glowed in the light of the oil lamp and she walked with purpose.

She entered Kelu's room and said, 'Everything's in order. Let's wait till midnight to act.'

Kelu sat on the cot, deep in thought. He felt warmth on his back and got startled. It was the girl. She was hugging him, and her bare upper body gave him warmth.

'What are you doing?' he asked.

'Thampra, if it was anyone else, they would have raped me tonight. Instead, you are giving me life. I submit myself to you with all my heart. I am all yours.'

Kelu gently asked her to move away from him.

'Girl, I am likely your father's age. I am married and not here to exploit your vulnerability. I am happy you are lucky enough to survive here without harm. I am hopeful, but not sure all these plans will work out tonight. We must stay focused.'

Silence crept into the room. Everyone sat in deep thought.

The girl was still sitting nearby Kelu, leaning on his shoulders. A few times, Kelu pushed her, but she stayed there.

Kelu realized she was probably feeling his fatherly love. He put his arm around her shoulder, and she smiled.

There was a knock at the door.

The woman got up in a hurry. She knew the time had come and opened the door. Outside were five of the oldest women.

Kelu realized they were a bunch he could trust. They rushed into the room. 'Now what?' one of them asked.

'Did you make sure those guys are all drunk?'

'Yes, Thampra. They will not wake up for two days guaranteed.'

'Okay. I need to go out, and get a few things from my cart, and then we can go to their rooms.'

The woman and the girl walked in the front, Kelu behind them, and the other women followed. They made as little noise as possible, but the doors were heavy, and some screeched a bit.

The woman was cautious at every door. Once they reached outside, Kelu ran to his cart. He pulled out the machete, axe, and dagger. He started to take the stone, then decided it was too heavy.

They went back inside, and the woman led Kelu to the first room. Inside, a man lounged on the cot with two girls beside him.

The girls screamed as Kelu stepped forward, dagger in hand. The man jolted upright, reaching for a nearby stick, but Kelu was faster.

He plunged the dagger deep into the man's throat. Blood spurted out violently, splattering across the room.

The man's hands shot up, gripping Kelu's arm in a futile attempt to push him away. His body convulsed, eyes wide with terror as he gasped for air, choking on his own blood. His legs kicked out, hitting the cot, rattling it as life drained from him.

The woman entered, moving past the chaos. She knelt by the trembling girls, her soft words easing their panic. Then, with cold fury, she turned to the man who lay dying, blood pooling beneath him.

'This is your day, bastard,' she hissed. 'I've been waiting twenty years for this. Your father raped me. Then you—and your friends.'

She spat in his face as the light in his eyes flickered out.

The girls pushed past Kelu, their movements frantic and driven by a fury he had never witnessed.

They fell upon the dying man, their small fists pummelling his body with brutal determination.

One girl bent down and bit into his arm, her teeth sinking into his flesh until blood dripped from her lips.

Another grabbed a broken piece of pottery from the floor—its jagged edge sharp enough to cut but blunt enough to drag pain—and used it to slice open his groin, mutilating him in ways that made Kelu's stomach churn.

The man groaned weakly, but there was no strength left in him to resist.

Kelu couldn't believe how much anger pulsed through these girls. They had suffered, yes, but to witness their rage unleashed like this was something he wasn't prepared for.

They were no longer girls—at that moment, they became wild animals, feeding on the violence like it was their only means of survival.

They moved from room to room, each time with the same brutal efficiency.

The two men in the next room barely stirred when the girls arrived, too drunk to understand the danger looming over them.

One lazily tried to push them away, but it was a feeble attempt, nothing that could stop the girls from carrying out their vengeance.

As the blows landed, his resistance died along with him. The same pottery shard was used again, cutting, stabbing, and leaving behind trails of blood in its wake.

When they had finished, when the last man had breathed his final, pitiful breath, Kelu stood in the doorway, frozen.

The girls, their faces expressionless, turned to him. 'I have one more thing to do,' he muttered, his voice barely above a whisper.

He left, disappearing into the night only to return moments later with the large stone. It was rough and heavy.

Without speaking, he entered the first room where the dying man lay. His face, already beaten and swollen, stared up at Kelu with vacant eyes.

Kelu lifted the stone above his head, his body trembling as he brought it down with all his strength.

Crack.

The sound of bone shattering echoed through the room, but Kelu wasn't done. He hit him again, harder, screaming, 'Why?'

Tears streamed down his face as he slammed the stone down over and over, even long after the man's head was unrecognizable.

The girls watched him, their eyes empty, and their hearts long dead to the violence around them. But Kelu was falling apart.

He was not like them. His emotions surged with every strike. His hands, covered in blood, slipped on the floor, but still, he didn't stop. He moved to the next room and did the same, smashing their skulls until blood and brain matter splattered across the walls.

His screams echoed in the narrow space, filled with agony, rage, and sorrow. 'Why?' he screamed again and again, each word more broken than the last.

When it was finally over, when every man had been reduced to nothing but lifeless bodies on the ground, Kelu collapsed onto his knees.

His chest heaved with sobs, his fingers stained crimson as he wiped them across his tear-streaked face.

The stone slipped from his grasp, clattering on the blood-soaked floor.

The girls stood over him, still silent, still watching, as if the violence had drained them of the last remnants of their humanity.

But Kelu—he had never felt more human, more fragile, more broken.

The oldest woman came forward and held him tight. 'It's over. Stop it. You did it, and you saved us all. Your brother died for us. Otherwise, we all would have rotted here. Does that not give you some peace?'

Kelu sat and calmed down. He thought about what the woman said. He realized they had blessed Vinay. His soul would go to heaven. He was the reason Kelu was here, saving these people.

He looked up and caught between sobs and laughter, tears streaming down his face as a strained, broken chuckle escaped his lips.

'Vinay, you bastard. I will see you when I see you. You are one of a kind, friend.'

The women around him cried. Some came forward and touched his feet out of respect. Some hugged him. Some kissed him.

They all showed respect in whatever way they knew how to. A few of them fainted, seeing all the blood.

Kelu told the woman to gather everyone. 'This is your day. You can all start a fresh life. Every one of you is free to leave.'

No one moved. They all had fears. Tomorrow morning, the story of this brutality would come out. Villagers would hunt for them, especially since the four who'd been killed were from wealthy, high caste.

Kelu told them to go toward his town. He said he would arrange shelter there, but it may take a few days. Until then, they would have to lay low.

Kelu took only the woman and the girl, as he'd promised. The rest of the women cried a lot. They left the house immediately before the sun rose.

They rushed through the unlit roads. The bullocks sensed Kelu's urgency, and pulled the cart as fast as possible.

The woman and the girl hid in the back of the cart under linen materials he carried to disguise himself as a merchant.

He felt like he was going on the same trip he'd made with Lakshmi before their marriage. His thoughts went back in time. Someone held his hands, and he did not move his hands.

'Lakshmi...'

Then he realized it was the girl. He hastened his hand away. She smiled at him. Kelu was not sure what to do. He continued his journey.

As the sun began to peek, he told the women to pull out clothes from the pile of linen and wear them. They needed to look like upper caste to survive further.

Once they were dressed, soon they could see a village. Many people were out in groups.

Kelu sensed danger. He did not stop the cart. He kept riding through the village.

The people stared at him and looked inside the cart. Kelu did not show any fear. The ladies just lay down, covering their faces under the linen. No one asked him to stop.

After a few minutes, Kelu felt his breath back and told them to sit up front.

The younger one sat close to him and said, 'Thampra, you are my saviour. I know you are an honourable man and married. I won't have a better life. Please take me home. I will be indebted to you forever.'

The older woman came forward and shoved her into the back of the cart.

'Stay there. I never thought you were this much of an opportunist. He's a married man. Yes, he saved you, but that doesn't mean he will ruin his life for you. You are still a slave; just remember that.'

Kelu said nothing.

They reached Pala in a few hours. He knew Lakshmi must be worried at home. He needed to send back news to her. He drove toward the warehouse.

He expected Kannan to be there to manage the inventory. At the warehouse entrance, they all stepped out of the cart.

Kelu looked around but could find no one. The warehouse seemed to be empty.

He turned to the women and said, 'Today onward, you both need to act like upper caste. You are mother and daughter. The names will be Rama and Sita. Is that clear?'

They both nodded.

Kelu walked into the warehouse, his footsteps echoing in the vast, empty space. At the far end, he saw Kannan standing, a lone figure amidst the shadows.

It had been months since Kelu had last seen him, and the man before him now looked like a ghost of the person he once knew.

The loss of Vinay had changed him. His face was gaunt, as if he hadn't slept in days. His eyes, sunken and rimmed with dark circles, stared vacantly at nothing. His shoulders slumped, weighed down by grief, and the once sturdy frame that carried the strength of a labourer now looked fragile, almost broken.

Kelu swallowed hard, trying to push down the sadness welling up inside him. He couldn't understand why the warehouse was empty, why it felt as though the air itself was heavy with loss. It had only been a few days since Vinay had been killed, but already, everything seemed to have unravelled.

'Kannan, is that you?' Kelu's voice was soft, hesitant.

Kannan turned slowly at the sound of his name, his face crumpling the moment he saw Kelu.

Tears welled in his eyes, and before Kelu could take another step, Kannan broke down, crying like a child who had lost everything.

His sobs filled the emptiness around them, raw and uncontrollable. Kelu rushed forward, pulling Kannan into his arms.

The man clung to him, his fingers digging into Kelu's shoulders as if he were the only thing keeping him tethered to this world.

Kelu held him tightly, his own chest heaving with emotion as tears began to spill from his eyes.

'Oh, Kannan...' he choked, his voice trembling. 'Son... your father was my brother. You are my son. I will take care of you and your family. Please, believe in me.'

He pulled back slightly, wiping the tears from Kannan's face with his rough hands, his voice thick with emotion. 'We will get through this together.'

Kannan collapsed onto the ground, his legs giving way beneath the weight of his grief. He buried his face in his hands, unable to stop the sobs that shook his body. Kelu knelt beside him, resting a hand on his shoulder, offering comfort in the only way he knew how—by being there.

No words could truly ease the pain, but his presence was steady, an anchor in the storm of Kannan's sorrow.

For a moment, they sat in silence, the only sound Kannan's muffled cries.

Then, through his tears, Kannan noticed something. He looked up, his eyes red and swollen, and saw feet standing behind Kelu.

Confusion furrowed his brow as he glanced up further and saw an old woman and a young lady standing there.

The woman's long black hair was tied in a loose braid, and her face bore a quiet strength, though her eyes carried a sadness of their own.

The younger lady, no older than eighteen, clung to her side, her large eyes wide as she stared back at Kannan.

Kannan looked to Kelu for an explanation, still too lost in his grief to comprehend what was happening.

Kelu stood and turned to face him. 'Kannan,' he said gently, 'this is Sita, and this is her daughter, Rama. They'll be staying here at the warehouse from now on. They'll work, and they'll be a big help to us.'

Kannan's eyes darted between them, still unsure, but he trusted Kelu enough not to question further. He didn't have the strength to.

Kelu said nothing about what had happened last night, and he had warned the women not to speak of it either. The fewer people who knew, the better their chances of survival.

Kannan wiped his face with the back of his hand, trying to regain some composure, though the grief still weighed heavily on him. He stood shakily and gestured toward the back of the warehouse.

'I'll show you the shower rooms,' he said, his voice barely above a whisper.

When he returned, Kelu said, 'Boy, cheer up. You are the man of the house now. You should make your father proud. I will be there for your every step.'

They walked out of the warehouse.

Kelu yelled, 'Ladies, we will get some food. Do not venture out.'

Kannan felt his energy coming back. They went to a nearby town and got food. When they returned to the warehouse, the women had showered and were waiting.

Sita glowed like a sun. Her smile was captivating. Kelu looked at Kannan, and he could see a gleam in the young man's eyes. He smiled inside.

***

Kelu started traveling to Pala once a month to oversee the business, training Kannan whenever he was there. Kannan liked Kelu's presence, and he told Kelu how much his father talked about him.

Kelu cried every time he saw Vinay's picture. Kelu wanted to make sure this family did well.

Rama and Sita helped in the shop, and they adapted quicker than Kelu expected. Kelu stayed in the shop overnight whenever he went there. Sita always tended to his needs.

Kannan ordered and selected the linen, and Kelu saw Vinay in him.

The way he walked, his smile, and even sometimes his voice. Kelu felt the presence of Vinay everywhere.

During one visit to Pala, Kannan told Kelu that Savitri was no longer leaving the house. She was not talking to anyone, not smiling anymore. Kannan did not know what to do.

Kelu promised he would convince Savitri to come out and be part of the business. Kelu knew how capable she could be. Vinay was successful because of Savitri's brain.

Kelu went to Vinay's house and knocked on the door.

No one answered.

He called out, 'Savitri, it's Kelu.'

He waited for a while, knocked again, and then pushed on the door. It was open. He saw Savitri sitting on the floor with her head on her knees.

'Savitri?' he said. She wouldn't look up. Kelu crouched in front of her. He could feel the pain lingering in the room. Savitri sobbed softly.

'Savitri, I know this was not fair. But it has been three months. You need to stand up for the family.'

Savitri cried louder. Kelu touched her hair and Savitri slowly looked up. Kelu began to cry as well.

They hugged and cried together for a while. So overcome with emotion were they, they did not realize they were hugging. Once they did, they leaped away from each other.

'Don't you dare take advantage of the situation!' Savitri was fuming.

Kelu was caught off guard by this. 'No, Savitri, please. Don't say that. Vinay was my brother.'

'Brother? Where have you been all this time? Three months later you finally come to see whether my son and I have died?'

'Savitri, please understand. I have been here with your son at the shop. I did not know what to say, and to tell you the truth, I was a coward. I couldn't face you. I know the pain. But I am here now. I want to be with you and support you.'

Savitri looked away and cried.

Kelu sat there and looked at her. She was so beautiful and lively when Vinay was around. Now look at her. She had aged so much. She was not taking care of herself.

Kelu went back to the store. He told Kannan he would come back next week.

Kelu was restless throughout the travel home. Upon his arrival, Kelu told Lakshmi what happened.

Lakshmi supported Kelu and told him to return to Pala and stay for a month. She knew Vinay's family needed support.

'They helped us so much. They are the reason we are together today.'

Kelu went to bed, and Lakshmi massaged his feet. He looked at Lakshmi and pulled her toward him.

She fell on his chest. The herbal oil on her hair always opened his senses.

Kelu kissed her forehead while his hands played the tunes he loved to play on her body. Their breaths synched, and their heartbeats became one rhythm. Kelu missed her lips.

Lakshmi's face was glowing. Kelu felt her stomach bump. He said, 'This will be our lineage carrier. Definitely a boy. I can see that.'

Lakshmi smiled. 'Good luck, Thampra. I think we will have a girl. But she will be a superpower. She will have all your temper and abilities. She will rule you.' Saying this, Lakshmi bit him playfully on his lip.

Kelu couldn't say anything back. They both laughed.

As morning arrived, Kelu opened his eyes. Lakshmi was still on his chest.

The sun peeped in through the top window, kissing her naked back.

Kelu saw a wound, as if someone tried to cut her. He couldn't believe what he saw. He didn't want her to wake up, so he lay there quietly. He could not believe this beautiful woman had married him.

He looked at her face, realizing how calm she looked. She was so beautiful. Any man would die for her. He wondered what had happened when he was away. Did someone attack her? Who would do this to a woman who was visibly pregnant?

He heard Narayani calling from the other room.

Kelu asked Lakshmi to move, then went and got Narayani. Just like her mom, she was happy to see Kelu and started giggling.

Narayani always wanted Kelu's presence. She started telling him about all the surprises she'd had while he was away.

Lakshmi joined them and reminded Kelu that it was okay for him to go back to Pala. She said she would take care of the business here.

'I saw the wound on your back. What happened?' Kelu asked.

'Oh, that. I was coming back from the pond.'

'Did someone attack you? Who was it?'

Lakshmi smiled. 'Calm down. Nothing like that. I just got cut by a branch. I didn't see it, as I was walking and looking back to see what Narayani was up to.'

Kelu didn't believe her. He could see the wound was not from a branch. It looked like it was from a sword or a dagger. Kelu looked at Lakshmi for a long time without speaking.

Finally, she got up and said, 'You need to go to Pala. Take care of your Vinay's family. I am fine here. Do not worry.' She hunched over and pulled his cheeks playfully. Narayani giggled.

Kelu could read Lakshmi's determination. But he wanted to make sure she was safe before he left for Pala. He called for two trusted workers.

'I want you both to be in the house until I return. I sense trouble here. Please make sure she is safe. Do anything, even if you have to kill someone. I will take care of you and your family. Is that clear?'

'Yes, Thampra. Don't worry, we will take care of Thampratti.'

Kelu returned to Pala. He told Kannan he would stay with them for a month at their house. Savitri was not too keen on this idea, and she threatened to leave home if Kelu stayed.

Kannan and Savitri argued. Kelu stood outside for a long time. He could hear things falling and breaking.

After a while, Kannan came out, took Kelu's bag and went in. Savitri was standing right by the door.

'You stay in that room,' she said, pointing toward her left. 'That's Kannan's room. You will not talk to me or come here in this living room.'

'I promised Vinay I would take care of his family if something like this happened. I refuse to stay in that room all the time, and I will talk to you, Savitri. Vinay is watching all this from heaven. Do not forget that. He would be happier if you moved on and gained some faith here.'

Savitri moved close to Kelu and tried to slap him. Kelu stopped her hand.

Kannan called out, 'Mother!' and started to move forward. Kelu stopped him with a gesture.

Savitri cried and pounded on Kelu's chest.

'Why, Kelu, why? God is so cruel. He took my happiness. I cannot live without Vinay. He got killed so brutal just for some money. I am so disgusted by you, Kelu. You are the reason. You brought this on us. You gave us this fortune. If you did not come in to our lives, Vinay would still be with me. You killed him. We may have been poor, but I am sure Vinay would still be with me.'

Kelu was devastated. He looked at Kannan, who looked away and cried.

Savitri kept hitting him. Finally, she got tired and hugged him. They both cried.

'Sorry,' Savitri said. 'I didn't know how to react. I know, Kelu, that it was not your fault. It's my fate,'

Looked at her face and said, 'You don't need to apologize. You said nothing bad here. I understand.'

Their eyes showed their pain, and silence crept in. Kannan fell asleep on the floor, tired. Kelu and Savitri sat on the floor, and then she lay on Kelu's lap. She slept there the whole night.

Kelu watched her sleep. This woman had lost all her hope. Vinay was a lucky man to have had a loving wife like her. But now, she needed to get up and be the backbone of her family. But how?

As Kelu's mind drifted, deep in thought, he moved his fingers through her hair. He could still see glimpses of her beauty here and there.

Savitri held his hand. Kelu was startled a bit. He did not want her to get mad. She was fully asleep, however, and unknowingly, she kissed his hand.

He wanted to stop her, but his emotions overcame his thoughts. She called him Vinay in her sleep. She slowly bit his fingers.

Kelu looked at Kannan, and then up on the wall. He saw Vinay's portrait, which Kannan had drawn, with a garland on it. Kelu felt Vinay's presence. He pulled his hand out of hers.

Savitri opened her eyes and bolted upright. She knew something was not right. She looked at Kelu and said, 'You should go to Kannan's room and sleep there.' She got up and went to her room.

Savitri couldn't sleep after that. She cried, and questioned god. She also did not want Kelu to stay with her. She would send someone to Lakshmi's to ask her to come and stay instead.

In the morning, Savitri came out of her room to find the house cleaned and tidied up. Vinay's portrait had a new garland. She also saw Kelu cleaning up the outside walls. She walked outside and asked Kelu what he wanted to eat.

Instead of answering, Kelu said, 'I know Vinay wanted to paint this house for a long time. I am here for a month, so I would like to do it, if that's okay with you?'

Savitri smiled at him and walked away. Kelu could sense she was ready to get back to her life.

Kannan arrived with milk. Kelu could see Vinay in him. He remembered his interaction with Vinay at the banks, where he spilt his milk.

Kannan saw his mother with a smile on her face. He looked at Kelu, then hugged him and said, 'I haven't seen my mother smiling like this since my father died. Thank you, Uncle, for doing this.'

Kelu worked hard all day. Savitri watched him from the kitchen window. She could see he was a robust man. She'd never looked at him like this before.

Kelu had an impressive physique. Vinay was not this strong. He never worked like this. Kelu looked at the window and saw her watching him. They looked at each other for a while.

Then Kannan came out, calling, 'Uncle, I will open the shop. I assume you are not coming today since you have a project already here. See you in the evening. Mother made nice idlis today. Please eat.'

Kelu washed his hands and went in.

Savitri came out with hot idlis and coconut chutney and served him. Kelu asked, 'Did you eat?'

'I will eat later. You eat now. You are the one who works out there, not me.'

Kelu smiled. 'You bring a plate and sit with me. I will serve you.'

Savitri wanted to say no, but she brought a plate and sat down with him. He served her. She held his hand, and Kelu said nothing.

She pulled his hand to her face and kissed his hand. Her eyes filled with tears. He reached out and wiped her tears. She leaned on his shoulder and cried. Kelu knew she was in a lot of pain.

'I know this is wrong,' Savitri said, 'but I want you. I miss Vinay a lot, but I cannot live like this. I see no one. Society has marked me as a widow. I may wear nothing colour. But I am not dead. I want to live. I am so lonely. I cannot talk about this to my son. I know only you and I want to trust you. Please do not leave me. I will not create problems for your family life. I want you to love me once. I want to live for my son, but I cannot live alone. My Vinay's memories are haunting me. The last two days, I am coming alive again because of your presence here. Please trust me.'

Kelu looked at Vinay's portrait. He felt Vinay smiling at him. He sensed everything was right at that moment. He held Savitri tight and whispered in her ear.

'I will be here for you. I will take care of you. Don't worry.'

Kelu couldn't believe his own words. He knew Lakshmi would never forgive him. He loved Lakshmi with a full heart, but what could he do?

Kelu kissed her forehead. Savitri took his face in her hands and kissed on his lips. Kelu was surprised by her actions. It was too fast for him. Yet, he did not stop her. He felt her lips on his.

She was crying and smiling. He would let her do what she wanted to do. She pushed him back onto the floor. The idly plate fell, and they laughed.

She lay on top of him and said, 'I never thought I would do this in my life. I always thought this was wrong. Now, though, I see the right in it. I am living again.'

She took her blouse off, and her breasts touched his chest. Kelu felt the warmth in her. Their time together was bliss.

When Kannan returned that evening, he saw Kelu had done nothing outside. 'Uncle, what happened? When I left, you were all ready to paint. Did you get tired? Or did Mother not let you do anything?'

Kelu and Savitri looked at each other. They both had the same expression on their faces. Savitri got up from the verandah and went inside. She didn't want to face Kannan.

Kelu smiled and said, 'My age was playing with me, son. I got lightheaded today. I will get at it tomorrow.'

'Please don't, Uncle. I was just asking. If you are not feeling well, this is not important for us now. Mother is smiling these days. I am thrilled.'

***

Meanwhile, Lakshmi was dealing with a troubling situation. A few of her acquaintances from childhood had figured out her escape and new identity. They saw an opportunity to loot her.

The cut she got was not from the branch, but from a dagger used by one attacker. She'd run from them, but Lakshmi knew she had to do something before the story about her got out.

One afternoon, a guy came to the house and walked into the courtyard. Lakshmi was outside watching Narayani play when she heard someone call out, 'Lakshmi.'

For a long time, no one other than Kelu called her that. She turned and couldn't believe her eyes. It was Panan, her neighbour's son from the old village.

'So,' he said, 'you are living here as a Thampratti, while back home we are struggling. How could you betray us and stay with a higher caste like this?'

Lakshmi told him to whisper so as not to alarm Narayani. She walked with him to the side of the house. There, she saw a few more familiar faces. Panan was not alone.

'You need to support my family,' Panan said. 'I need money. If not, I will let everyone here know about your past.'

Lakshmi knew she needed to act quickly. 'Panan, I am living here with little in my control. My husband takes care of everything. I don't think, I could do much for you.'

'Then get your husband. I am sure he's clever. He can give us what we want to keep us quiet.'

'You don't know my husband, Panan. He would kill you all, with no one knowing. Better you leave me and my family alone.'

'No. You have one day to arrange money for us. We will not be nice anymore after that. Last time you ran off, but this time, you won't escape. Don't think we don't know how to cut you up. This time we will, if you don't give us what we want. The six of us will wait by the bush near the pond. Send us a message once you're ready with the money. And remember, if you try to act smart, we have nothing to lose here. We'll make sure this village turns against you and your husband. Act wisely.'

He walked away with a smirk on his face, the threat hanging in the air like a dark cloud.

Lakshmi stood frozen for a moment, her heart pounding in her chest. She grabbed Narayani's hand and hurried inside the house.

Once they were safe inside, she released the little girl, her hands trembling as she locked the door behind them.

The weight of the threat bore down on her like a boulder, crushing her under its weight. She began pacing the small room, her thoughts spinning out of control.

What if they told the village? What if her past, her parents, her sister's shame, all of it came spilling out in one awful moment?

She could see the disgust on the faces of the villagers, the whispers behind her back, the cruel judgment. Her child—how would she bear it? And Kelu—where was Kelu when she needed him most?

She wished he were here, his strong arms around her, his voice steadying her trembling heart. He would know what to do. He always knew what to do. But he wasn't here, and she was alone.

She pressed her fingers against her temples, feeling the pulse of a headache beginning to form. Her mind raced with possibilities, but none of them offered a way out. What if they didn't believe her? What if they turned against her, just like he said? How would she protect Narayani?

Her thoughts spiralled further into panic, her breathing quick and shallow. She felt the walls closing in, the weight of her secret threatening to crush her.

Kelu's mother, noticing her daughter-in-law's distress, stepped into the room quietly.

'Lakshmi, are you all right, my dear?' she asked, her voice gentle but filled with concern. 'I've never seen you this worried. I know your husband is away, and you've been handling everything on your own, but you don't have to carry this burden alone. Can I help you with anything, dear?'

Lakshmi turned to her mother-in-law, her face pale and drawn. She tried to speak, but the words caught in her throat. She felt like she was drowning, suffocating under the pressure of the threat. How could she explain this? How could she put this weight on her?

'No, Mother. Please just take care of Narayani. I need to go out and arrange for some people to send some linen urgently. I will get two workers to come to town with me.'

Kelu's mom was not happy. 'That idiot Kelu should be here, not out there taking care of someone else's family and business.'

Lakshmi went and talked to the workers Kelu had asked to stay with her. 'There are a few people here in town. They wanted to attack us. I believe they are Kelu's enemies. They came here when you guys went off for your lunch. They tried to warn me, but I think we need to teach them a lesson before it's too late,'

The men would do anything for Kelu, who had always treated them well.

Lakshmi said, 'There are six people, and we need to do everything subtly. What I am thinking is not to attack them with weapons, but to poison them.'

She was shivering with anger. She knew there was no room for error, but her motherly instinct and love for her family drove her. She decided to take a chance and go with the plan.

She ordered a grand meal from a nearby place and asked the workers to get those men from their hideout.

She mixed the food with some poison and waited outside for them to come. She wanted to make sure all six came together.

When they arrived, there were only five.

'You said there were six of you.'

'One went back to the village because his son is not well. We will give him the share he deserves.'

'No, you need to bring him as well. I do not want another visitor asking for money.'

Panan looked upset. 'It's impossible. He left right after we met this afternoon.'

Lakshmi had no choice but to move forward. She knew the danger; the guy could come back looking for his friends and money. But it was too late now. She went with the plan.

'Guys, come in. I have some food for you to eat. And I have the money.'

Panan refused to eat. 'Just give us the money and we will leave.'

'No, Panan, you are like my older brother. You took care of me when I was a child. You need to eat,' Lakshmi insisted.

He relented and they all went into the outbuilding, where Lakshmi served them poisoned food. She knew within a few minutes; they would all be dead.

She excused herself, saying she had to go get the money, and went back to the kitchen.

She waited there, and cried. She was one of them. She had sworn to help low-caste people.

But she was killing them now. She couldn't believe how cruel she had become.

She touched her stomach and prayed. 'God, please don't make my child suffer for this, but I need to save my family.'

An hour passed, and Lakshmi could barely contain the storm brewing inside her. She sent a few workers to see what had become of Panan and his friends. They returned shortly, their faces pale, and confirmed— Panan and the others were dead.

Lakshmi gave the orders with a hollow voice, instructing them to take care of the bodies and, above all, not to say a word to Kelu.

As soon as they left, she broke down. Her legs felt weak as she walked back toward the main house, her chest tightening with every step. Hot tears spilled down her face, blurring her vision as memories of Panan flooded her mind.

He wasn't always like this, she reminded herself. There was a time when Panan had been kind, a friend, almost like family. When they were young, Panan had looked out for her.

She remembered when her father had been too sick to work, how Panan had come by their small home with baskets of food. He'd never asked for anything in return. Back then, his smile was warm, a boy with a good heart who had grown up too fast in a world too cruel.

She recalled the rainy season, years ago, when the roads had flooded, and no one could travel. Her family had been stranded, cut off from the market, and the little food they had was quickly running out.

It was Panan who had shown up, drenched from head to toe, carrying sacks of rice and vegetables on his back. 'You're like a sister to me,' he'd said with a grin, waving off her thanks. 'This is nothing.'

And there were the smaller things, too—like when he helped her fetch water from the river, carrying the heavy pots for her without complaint, or the time he had defended her when a group of boys taunted her for being poor.

Panan had been her protector then, her friend when few others had cared. But now... now she had killed him.

Lakshmi couldn't comprehend how life had twisted into this nightmare. How had they come to this? Panan had turned into someone unrecognizable, corrupted by greed and desperation.

And now, because of her choices, he was dead. She had repaid his kindness with death. The thought made her sick, twisting her stomach into knots as guilt tore at her heart.

She paused just outside the house, wiping her tear-streaked face with trembling hands. What had she become? She couldn't deny it anymore.

The girl who had once been grateful for Panan's friendship was gone, replaced by a woman capable of orchestrating his death.

The weight of it all crushed her. She wanted to scream, to tear at her clothes, to do something, anything, to erase what had happened. But there was no going back. Panan was dead. And she was the one who had caused it.

Kelu's mother was waiting outside. 'You took so long, dear. It worried me. Narayani cried a little to see you before she went to bed. I am not liking this; you are working way too much when you are pregnant. You need to get Kelu back here.'

Lakshmi said nothing and continued inside.

She did not sleep the whole night, wondering if the other guy would come back. She cursed herself for acting without asking Kelu.

She turned and looked at Narayani, who was in a deep sleep. The moonlight on her face gave her innocent beauty. Lakshmi went to her and held her, finally falling asleep herself.

The following morning, she met with the workers and made sure they'd disposed of the bodies with no trouble. She offered them some money, but they refused.

'We would do anything for Kelu Thampra. His family is like ours. Thampratti, yesterday you were asking about a sixth person. We need to find him. We cannot have loose ends here.'

'I agree, but I don't know who he is or where he was from. We need to lay low and wait until he shows up. I am sure he will be back to see why his friends did not return. I know what to do then.'

She did not show the fear she felt. She knew how to behave in front of others. She needed to guide them.

***

Two days passed, and no one showed up. Lakshmi stayed alert, her knife always within reach. She slept lightly, if at all, waking at the slightest noise.

The silence was unnerving, pressing down on her as the hours dragged by. The tension in her body never eased—each passing minute without a visitor only sharpened her wariness. She had expected someone by now.

On the third evening, just as the last of the sunlight dipped below the horizon, a figure appeared at the gate. Lakshmi's grip tightened on the knife at her waist.

A boy stood there, no more than fifteen. His thin frame was hunched, uncertainty in every line of his body. He looked out of place, his bare feet dirty from the road, and his eyes wide with worry as he glanced around, perhaps wondering if he should even be here.

His skin, rough and darkened from the sun, seemed to blend with the earth around him, and his clothes— if they could be called that—hung loosely on him.

He wore only a simple, coarse loincloth, the fabric fraying at the edges.

A thin, worn shawl was draped over his shoulder, the kind that offered little protection against the wind or cold. His hair was matted with dirt and sweat, sticking to his forehead in uneven clumps.

He shifted on his feet, his gaze flitting between Lakshmi and the ground, as though afraid to meet her eyes for too long.

Lakshmi said nothing at first, watching him closely. She had been on edge for days, and now, standing before her was this boy—a low-caste labourer, judging by his appearance. He looked nervous, like he knew he didn't belong here but had nowhere else to go.

'Can I talk to Lakshmi Thampratti please?'

'That is me, how can I help you.'

'I am Panan's nephew. He came here few days ago but he never came back. I cannot find him.'

'Panan?' She tried not to cry. 'Who is he? I don't know him.'

'He told me everything before he came here. I know he and his friends were here. I need to talk to him. If you don't allow me to or tell me where he is, I will tell everyone about your past.'

Here we go again, Lakshmi thought. She could not kill him, though; he was only a kid himself. Lakshmi tried to reason with him.

'I haven't met with Panan, or his friends. I am not sure you have the right place here. It must be in some other village.'

'No. You are lying,' said a female voice.

Lakshmi turned and saw Nanamma, Panan's sister, standing in the doorway. For a moment, it felt as if the earth beneath her shifted. Unease prickled at her, but she quickly composed herself, her grip instinctively tightening around the knife at her waist.

'Who are you?' Lakshmi demanded; her voice sharp.

Nanamma sneered, a flicker of something dark in her eyes.

'You don't remember me? I used to play with you when you were one of us. Before you became what you are now. Look at you. You've forgotten your roots. Your nature has changed. You live among those who defile our women every day.'

Lakshmi's face hardened. She stepped closer, closing the gap between them, her movements deliberate and unflinching.

'You need to shut up,' she said in a low, threatening tone, pulling the knife from her waist, its blade gleaming faintly in the dim light. 'I am not the girl you think you know.'

At that moment, Kelu's trusted workers arrived. Without taking her eyes off Nanamma, Lakshmi gave an order. 'Take her and her son to the outbuilding.'

As Nanamma and the boy were led away, Lakshmi turned back toward the main house, her mind racing. This wasn't part of the plan. She had to act, but carefully.

After pacing the great hall for what felt like hours, she made up her mind. The truth was the only weapon she had left. She called the workers back, her voice firm. 'Bring them here. Into the great hall.'

Nanamma and her son were ushered in, their faces pale with fear. The boy clung to his mother's side, and Nanamma, for the first time since she'd arrived, looked shaken.

'Please, Lakshmi,' she whispered, her defiance gone, 'don't hurt us.'

Lakshmi crossed her arms, her gaze hard as she sized up Nanamma. She looked older now, more fragile than Lakshmi remembered. There was a desperation in her eyes, a far cry from the bold woman who had stood at the doorway minutes before.

Nanamma's clothes were worn, much like the boy's—simple, threadbare garments that spoke of a life much harder than Lakshmi's now. Yet there was still something bitter in her stare, an edge that reminded Lakshmi of the village they had both once called home.

'You think I've changed?' Lakshmi's voice was cold, measured. 'Yes, I am the one you knew. But I'm not the one destroying lives—you are. I could help you, Nanamma. You could live here, with me. Your son could work in our linen business, and you would want for nothing. But if you've come here like Panan, to drag me back into ruin, I won't spare you.'

Nanamma flinched at the mention of her brother, and Lakshmi continued, her tone softening just slightly. 'You should be happy, Nanamma. One family from our neighbourhood escaped. But instead, you and your family would rather pull us back down. How is that fair?'

Nanamma's silence was answer enough. Nanamma kneeled in front of Lakshmi and cried. 'So, you killed my brother. Why should I trust you now?'

'Look around my house. I have only fellows from low caste working here. Why? I am their saviour. Yes, I have a noble life, but I am trying to support my kind. Instead, you and your brother are calling me a rapist. My husband, whenever he has time, helps low-caste women. You should be ashamed.'

Lakshmi started to leave.

Nanamma and her son grabbed at her legs. 'Please help us. We will work here.'

'Okay, you may stay here and work. Now, tell me who was the guy who returned to your village? Panan said there were six, but I saw only five. Do you know who he is?'

'Yes, Thampratti, I know him. He is not a righteous man. He's the reason Panan came here. At first, Panan didn't want to ruin your life. But he persuaded him.'

'Well, I need your help to take care of him. My workers will go with your son to the village. He should show them who the man is. They will take care of the rest.'

Lakshmi called the workers and explained what needed to happen. They left that afternoon. Lakshmi felt a little relief, and she slept that night peacefully.

Nanamma took care of Kelu's mother's needs and they became close. Lakshmi kept Nanamma away from Narayani, and also away from the kitchen. She always had an eye on her. She suspected that one day, Nanamma could try to take revenge on them.

A few days later, Kelu's mother fell gravely ill. The change came quickly—too quickly for anyone to prepare.

Lakshmi had noticed her health faltering for weeks, perhaps even months, but this was different. The old woman could no longer rise from her bed, her breath shallow, her once-sharp eyes clouded with pain. Lakshmi had seen it before—the slow decline of a body worn out by years of hard labour and a lifetime of sorrow. She knew the signs. The end was near.

She wasted no time. Lakshmi sent word to Kelu, knowing he would want to see his mother before it was too late.

When Kelu arrived, the house felt different, as if a heaviness hung in the air. His heart sank the moment he saw his mother lying on the low wooden cot, barely able to turn her head to look at him.

Her skin had taken on a greyish pallor, and her breathing was ragged, as if each breath was a battle she might lose.

The strong, determined woman who had raised him was fading, her body shrinking under the weight of the illness that had quietly eaten away at her for so long.

Kelu knelt beside her, his chest tightening with the ache of seeing her this way. 'Amma,' he whispered, but she barely stirred.

Her eyes fluttered open, her hand trembling as she reached for his. The touch was weak, a shadow of the firmness it once had. He gripped her hand tightly, his thumb tracing the rough lines of her skin, the calluses formed by years of toil.

For days, Kelu rarely left her side. He brought her water, fed her when she could still take in food, and sat with her in silence as she drifted in and out of consciousness.

Their conversations were sparse, but the few words she managed to say were filled with warmth. She told him she was proud, that she was ready.

Kelu struggled to reply, his voice choking with unspoken grief. It felt too soon. He wasn't ready to say goodbye.

By the time the end came, it felt as though a part of him had been hollowed out. His mother passed peacefully, with Kelu by her side, just days after his return.

The days that followed were a blur of funeral rites and religious ceremonies. Kelu went through the motions, but his mind was elsewhere.

After the cremation, he retreated to the verandah, sitting in the corner as he had done so many times before as a child, but now the silence weighed heavily on him. Vinay and his mother—both gone, both pillars of his life—left a void he couldn't fill. Even Narayani's bright presence couldn't pull him out of the haze that clouded his thoughts.

Lakshmi watched him from a distance, knowing he needed something—perhaps more than she could give him. She gently suggested he return to Pala.

He resisted at first, but deep down, Kelu knew she was right. He needed a change, a way to fill the emptiness that had settled into his heart.

He'd only been back a few weeks when he was informed Lakshmi was showing signs of going into labour. Any day now, Kelu could be a father.

Lakshmi asked him to return as soon as he could. Kelu was elated. He couldn't contain his happiness and he let out a shriek. Kannan came running, only halfway dressed.

Kelu yelped again. 'I will be a father in a few days. I am sure this will be our son.' Kelu hugged Kannan and then walked to the kitchen.

He was looking for Savitri. She was sitting on the floor, scrapping coconut. Her waist cloth was pulled above her knees and Kelu could see her thighs. She got up right away, as she saw Kannan was with him.

Kannan blurted out the news.

Savitri was sad. Not because of him becoming a father, but because she knew Kelu needed to go. His priority and responsibility would always lie with Lakshmi.

Kelu had been home for a week, but the baby still hadn't arrived. The tension in the house was thick. Lakshmi was heavily pregnant, her body strained not only by the impending birth but by the weight of everything around her—the deaths, the enemies lurking in the shadows, and the constant presence of those who had reason to resent her. She hadn't spoken directly about it, but Kelu could sense her need for him.

This time, there was no way Lakshmi would send him back to Pala. Not now. She needed him by her side.

Kelu convinced her that he needed to go back for a bit due to Kannan's inability to negotiate a new deal they are working on. Yet Kelu had never told Lakshmi the full truth about his life in Pala.

Savitri no longer needed him. She was doing well, managing on her own, but Kelu enjoyed the life he had built there—the business, the thrill of playing both sides, and the satisfaction of guiding Kannan through the market's pitfalls.

Kelu had been teaching Kannan how to negotiate, helping him navigate the complexities of the linen trade, especially with Vinay's death still casting a shadow over their dealings.

Kannan was eager but inexperienced, and without Kelu, the boy would have been easy prey for unscrupulous traders.

One day, as Kelu and Kannan were discussing prices at a store, Krishnan arrived. Kelu hadn't seen him in a long time—not since before Lakshmi had given birth to their first child.

Krishnan, carried his years well. Despite being in his late eighties, he still had a vitality that made it easy to forget his age. He had come to see Kelu, not for business, but for family matters.

'Appa,' Kelu greeted him, a mix of respect and affection in his voice. It was rare for Krishnan to come down to Pala, as he had been busy managing the branches of Vinay's business. His daughters, Lakshmi's sisters, worked closely with him, helping run everything smoothly. Krishnan, despite his age, was still sharp and quick-witted. The businesses thrived under his guidance, and he was earning well.

'Let's sit,' Krishnan said, his tone calm but firm. Kelu led him inside, away from the bustle of the market.

Kelu had been thinking about this moment for some time.

'Appa, we need to talk,' he began. 'Kannan is learning, but he still needs guidance. You know how ruthless these traders can be. He can't do this alone.'

Krishnan listened carefully, his brow furrowing slightly. He had always trusted Kelu, but he could sense something deeper in his son-in-law's words.

'I can't always be here,' Kelu continued. 'You should consider moving back to Vinay's town. Kannan needs someone like you, someone who can mould him and help him become what Vinay intended. With you there, I can focus on what needs to be done here.'

'What's wrong with you?' Krishnan said. 'You should let that family go now. This business was all your setup. You should run this and let your wife and kids enjoy it. Your sister-in-law also has a family now. So why you are so invested in Kannan? Give him some money and let them go do what they want.'

Kelu was livid. He pushed Krishnan to the wall and reminded him of his own past. 'Because of this family you are living the life you have now. Never forget that.' Kelu was shaking in anger.

Krishnan left. He was not at all pleased with Kelu. Krishnan decided to visit Kelu's house.

Lakshmi was surprised to see her father, but happy to see him. She went to him and hugged him, asking for his blessings for the baby, which was due any day now. Krishnan said nothing back.

Lakshmi knew right away something was wrong. She released the hug and sat in a nearby chair.

'Is everything okay, Father? Is Kelu doing well?'

'Do not say a word about Kelu. Do not even say his name. I do not want to hear about him. His wife is pregnant here, but he's playing the family man there. Who knows what he's doing with that girl there.'

'Which girl, Father? What are you talking about? Why are you so upset? Please, tell me what has happened. You are not helping me here. I am getting worried.'

Krishnan knew exactly what he was doing— pushing poison into Lakshmi's heart.

'Who else? Savitri. He's staying in their house. They take advantage of his good heart. Why don't you ask him to come back here? I don't understand the need here for him to spend so many days there.'

'Do not forget about our past. Kelu is the reason we are here. He is an unselfish man who is helping his friend's family. What's wrong with that? Are you losing your mind? Please do not talk like that about my husband again. Is that the reason you came here today? I was happy. I thought you came all this way to see me or help me. But you came here to complain about this? You should be ashamed. I don't want to see you. Please go away.'

Krishnan had not expected his daughter to react like this. He yelled at her, 'You will regret this one day, my daughter. You will. I am leaving now. I don't want to stay here either. You do not respect me. Do not come crying to me later. I will not give you shelter. They will change Kelu. I can see it. You are a foolish woman not to see it.'

He took the water pan by the entrance and threw it away.

Lakshmi did not say a word. She cried while walking back to her room. She tried not to get affected by her father's words. But why had he come? Was there a reason? Did he really see something there? Slowly, the poison he'd planted worked on her.

Lakshmi got worried. She lay down, crying until it grew dark. Narayani came in asking for food. Lakshmi led her out to feed her and saw Krishnan still there. She went up to him.

'Father, did you eat?'

'No, I will eat with Narayani.' Krishnan looked at Lakshmi and said, 'Daughter, you cannot be this naïve. You need to control him. This wealth of his belongs to you and your family. He should not toil for some other family. Yes, Vinay helped you a lot. But that is past. Kelu cannot be there forever. He should work for you and your sisters. We are his family. You should call him back and ask him to take control of Vinay's business. Pay Kannan only a salary to live. That is how it should be.'

'Father, I am not worried about the money. I am worried about what you implied he is doing with Savitri.'

'She is a widow. And she is brilliant, not naïve like you. She can easily persuade men.'

'Father, I know my Kelu, He would do nothing bad to me or his friend Vinay. He loves both of us dearly.

I am sure he respects Savitri, and treats Kannan as his son. One more thing, Father. I am very content with what I have. Kelu loves me and he provides me shelter, excellent food, and now soon, two kids. What more could I ask from him? Especially when he provided everything I have to my sisters and parents, too.'

Krishnan got up very upset. 'I am leaving, and I will not come back again to help you. I did my job here to warn you. God bless you and your children.'

Lakshmi watched her father walk away. She knew her family's harmony was in danger. The air had a bitter taste now. She was worried. Narayani came running. She wanted to play with her grandfather.

Lakshmi told her to go and wait for food. Narayani could sense her mother's anger and did not argue.

Lakshmi went to the prayer room, where she stood before the goddess Parvathi. 'Mother, you helped me so far. I am from a low-caste family, yet you gave me this house, a husband who loves me, a beautiful daughter, and now I will have another baby. Please help me preserve what we have. I want clarity. Please, Mother, don't let my thoughts wander. Please give me the strength to fight this uncertainty. I love my family. Please, Mother, please.'

She cried and sat in front of the picture. After a while, she was shaken by Narayani's voice asking for food again.

This time, with some determination, Lakshmi got up. She had changed. She quickly fed her daughter and then sent her to bed.

Lakshmi's thoughts turned to her mother. How much she had suffered at the hands of the upper caste. She remembered her mother crying daily because of an individual who always harassed her at work.

She often heard her mother talking to her father, pleading with him not to send her back to work. But her father was always after money. He never listened.

Once, she saw her mother changing. Her breasts had bite marks, and her back had traces of beatings. Lakshmi didn't understand what was happening to her mother.

One day, Lakshmi went to see her mother at work. She saw her mother tied to a pole. A man was standing in front of her and hitting her hard.

Lakshmi got scared. She was young, but she knew if she went in there she would be beaten too. She ran to her father, but he did nothing. His behaviour surprised her.

That evening, Lakshmi sat with her mom and asked her what had happened. As her mother explained, she realized her life could be the same one day. She started praying to the Goddess Parvathi from then onward.

Lakshmi couldn't shake the memories her father had stirred up. Everything she had tried to bury was resurfacing—her old life, the struggles, the scars.

It felt like a lifetime ago, but now, with her father's presence, it was all creeping back into her mind.

She found herself watching Kelu more closely, wondering if he too would start to change, if the pull of power and privilege would shift him. All high-caste men were the same, she thought bitterly. They used women like her, always did.

Lakshmi's actions had become quieter, more calculating. She no longer spoke with the same fire she once had, but her silence held weight. She found herself withdrawing from the others, observing them more than participating.

She still carried the knife at her waist, but now it felt heavier, a reminder of who she had become and what she had left behind.

The distance between her and Kelu grew, not because of words, but because of everything unsaid. There was a quiet shift in Lakshmi, a hardness that hadn't been there before. She could feel it.

***

In Pala, Kelu painted the house. Kannan helped him every evening. He enjoyed Kelu's company, and he started not to miss Vinay as much.

Savitri continued to bloom. She got much more involved with the business and Kannan's needs.

Kelu never really spent time with her anymore. He was busy with Kannan and his own establishments.

Two weeks went by, and the time neared for Kelu's departure. Kannan was becoming confident in his own abilities.

He told Kelu, 'Uncle, I can run this business. I am thrilled that you taught me. I don't know how to thank you for doing this. I would have lost my mother, but you brought her and my future back. I will be there for you. I dedicate my entire life to you. This is my word. I would die for you.'

Savitri was listening from inside. She came out with tears rolling down her cheeks. She hugged her son and told him, 'Don't you ever think that you would lose me. Yes, I was going through a tough time, but never would I have let you go. You can count on me.'

She turned to Kelu. 'You are a powerful force for us. Please come whenever you can. I will stay strong, though I will miss your help here for sure.'

Kelu wanted to hug her, but Kannan was there, so he controlled himself.

As Kelu was trying to sleep that night, he heard someone come into the room. 'Who is it?'

'It's me, Savitri. Please don't talk. Kannan is still awake.'

Kelu said nothing. She sat by him on the bed. It was dark, but Kelu could see her glowing eyes. He could also smell the herbal oil she used on her hair. The aroma of it always aroused him. Neither of them talked. Their breath filled the room. They never moved, and they never touched.

After some time, Kelu reached out his hand to feel where she was. No one was there. He got up and put an oil lamp on. Had Savitri really come, or was it all in his head? He wanted to go to her room. He became restless and paced in the room.

'You cannot sleep.'

He turned upon hearing the abrupt voice and saw Savitri standing by the door.

'Kelu, I cannot ruin your life. I was a wife too. I know how Lakshmi will feel if she finds out about us. You need to forget about me. I will be fine here. Thank you so much for everything you have done for me and my son.'

Kelu moved forward and held her hands. Savitri did not deny him. 'You deserve more,' he said.

Kelu pulled her toward him, and she moved per his wishes. He pushed her to the wall and leaned his body on her. Kissed her head and neck and felt her melting into his arms. He moved her to the bed and they indulged their passion.

Savitri cried throughout the bliss and Kelu wiped her tears. They both knew this would not last forever.

As they lay together afterwards, Savitri said, 'You should never come back here. Ever. If you love me and my son, stay away from us. I am happy the way I am now.'

Kelu said nothing in return, but held her tighter. They lay together till the sun came up.

'Mother, where are you?' Kannan called.

Savitri got up in a hurry, and Kelu saw her in sunlight for the first time with no clothes on. She got shy and pulled on her clothes quickly. She got ready and went toward the door but then stopped. What if Kannan was standing there?

She turned and asked Kelu to go out first, and if Kannan was there, to divert his attention.

Kelu smiled and said, 'It's okay, let him find out about us. What does it matter?'

Savitri stared at him. Kelu got up and pinched her while walking toward the door with a mischievous smile on his face. He told her to come out, and Savitri quickly went to the kitchen.

Kelu went to the well. Kannan was there.

'Did you see my mother? I usually wake her up for making breakfast, but today she was not in her bed.'

'She was in the kitchen when I was coming out just now.'

'Really, today there will be rain and thunder for sure? First time she's done this. My father or I have always had to wake her up. Strange.'

Kannan laughed and headed in. 'Uncle, come in quick. She will make a delicious breakfast. You are leaving today, so you won't get another chance for the delicious food my mother makes.'

Kelu suddenly felt like he was moving out of his own home, and he struggled to control his emotions. He kept telling himself that he had a family, that he would be a father again soon.

That his responsibilities were higher than what he had now and he needed to leave.

That afternoon, Kelu started packing. He paused in between. He was hyperventilating. His conscious mind was not stable. He packed again.

He could see Savitri outside clearing debris using a coconut leaf broom. He went closer to the window and watched her for a while. She turned and looked toward the window. He got startled momentarily, then regained his composure.

He went back to packing. He realized he needed to hurry, that Kannan could come at any time with his bullock cart to pick him up.

***

Back at the bungalow, Lakshmi paced the floor, her swollen belly making each step feel heavier than the last. Her body was tired, her emotions frayed, but tonight, excitement mingled with her unease.

Kelu was finally coming back. She had made up her mind—this time, she wouldn't let him leave again. She couldn't.

The baby was due any day now, and her heart ached for his presence, even more so after the unsettling meeting with her father.

The pregnancy had taken a toll on her in more ways than she had expected. One moment she was filled with hope, and the next, she was drowning in anxiety.

Late that night, Kelu arrived, his face drawn and weary. The travel had clearly drained him, and there was something off in the way he moved, sluggish and weak. He barely acknowledged Lakshmi's presence. His eyes were glazed with exhaustion, and he muttered something about feeling unwell before heading straight to bed without so much as a glance at their daughter.

Lakshmi's heart sank. She had been waiting all evening, her mind buzzing with things to say, but all her words dissolved into the thick silence between them.

'Have you eaten?' she asked, her voice soft, almost pleading.

He barely nodded, but the answer didn't matter. He was already asleep the moment he collapsed onto the bed.

Lakshmi stood by the bedside, watching him. The joy she had felt earlier was slipping away, replaced by a growing sense of dread. She had missed him terribly, and yet, here he was, so distant it felt like a stranger lying in her bed.

He hadn't even embraced her, hadn't asked about the baby or how she was doing. The realization stung, and without warning, tears welled up in her eyes.

Was her father right all along? Were all men like this—taking what they wanted, and then withdrawing into their own lives?

Krishnan's words replayed in her mind, twisting her thoughts into knots.

She could see the truth in them now, but she didn't want to believe it. Not about Kelu. He was different. He had to be.

The night stretched on, but Lakshmi couldn't sleep. She stayed awake, her mind restless, glancing occasionally at Kelu's sleeping form.

Her hand moved instinctively to her belly, feeling the baby's kicks—a reminder that time was running out. She needed to talk to him, to ask him if he had truly changed. But now wasn't the time, and maybe, she thought bitterly, there would never be a time.

Then there was the lingering fear—Nanamma, Panan's sister, still working in the household, her presence a constant reminder of the killings.

Lakshmi wanted to tell Kelu everything, to unburden herself of the secret that had been weighing on her since that day. But each time the thought crossed her mind, something stopped her. What would Kelu say? Would he still stand by her? Or would he turn away like so many others had?

Lakshmi spent the night battling these thoughts, her mind a storm of worry, guilt, and the painful reality that things were slipping beyond her control. Even in the dark, with her husband mere inches away, she had never felt more alone.

Lakshmi was carrying her second child. Both husband and wife prayed hard to get blessed with a boy.

Kelu wanted to teach him all the business tricks he'd learned. He wanted him to be the leader of the town. He couldn't wait for his arrival.

Finally, the day arrived. Lakshmi was in pain. She usually brushed off her hardships, but this time, it was different.

Kelu got worried. He still could not bear to see tears in her eyes. He was the reason they took so long to conceive another child; he could not bear to see her go through the birthing pain again.

Kelu called a midwife to the house. He stayed inside the room for a while, but then the midwife told him to go out and wait. He paced on the verandah. Narayani was playing outside. He was so restless.

He went back into the room several times, but the midwife kicked him out each time, finally locking the door. Despite the pain, Lakshmi laughed a little.

After what seemed like forever, the sound of a cry came. Kelu rushed toward the room.

The midwife came out with the baby in her hands. 'Congratulations. You have a baby girl.'

Kelu stopped for a moment. He'd wanted a boy, and initially, the news disappointed him. Then he realized she was god's gift.

He took her in his arms. She was beautiful, and she was a hundred percent, Lakshmi. Her forehead, her lips, her cheeks. She even got a mole right under her breast area. She was a carbon copy of Lakshmi.

'How is Lakshmi?'

'She is doing well. You can go in.'

Kelu stepped in and saw Lakshmi in bed. She looked exhausted.

'Dear,' she said, 'I am sorry I couldn't give you a boy.'

'Never be sorry. I am so happy. Did you look at her? She looks exactly like you. Now I have three angels in my house. I need a guard so no guys will eye on you three… ha ha.'

'I am thrilled, Lakshmi.' He kissed her forehead. 'I have a name for her.'

'Let me hear what you have in mind.'

'We will name her Bhavani.'

As they hugged, Lakshmi cried silently. She knew Kelu was hiding something from her.

***

Part Three: Surya

Dogs howled outside. Kelu realized it was late in the night. It was getting cold, so he got up and closed the window. He went back to bed and tried to close his eyes, but he couldn't sleep. The memories flowed again.

Narayani was now eighteen and Bhavani fifteen. Kelu's reputation had traveled all over the country. He had no competition in his linen business. He proudly believed his girls were lucky for him.

He traveled a lot, and Lakshmi never had a say in his decisions. She knew society respected him and his decisions were final. However, Lakshmi wanted her daughters to be strong and taught them how to stand up for their rights.

Out of the two, Bhavani was very strong willed. She was just like Kelu. She could make decisions and execute them at a very young age. Narayani was a very sweet, sensitive girl. Lakshmi knew Bhavani would handle the family if something went wrong.

Lakshmi had a few workers who she trusted the most. They traveled with Kelu, especially when he traveled to Pala. She had them keep a close eye on him whenever he visited Pala.

To this day, however, no one had said anything bad about Kelu, except Krishnan. Lakshmi never had a reason to suspect Savitri, still, she never let her guard down.

Kannan fell in love with Sita.

Savitri knew Sita was low caste, but she was happy to accept her as daughter-in-law. She felt the decision would thrill Vinay, his son accepting a low-caste woman.

The news excited Lakshmi. She and Kelu went to Pala with their daughters for the wedding, which was extravagant. Krishnan was not at all happy with the luxurious wedding.

Kelu took care of everything. As he had had no son of his own, he considered Kannan his son. There were four elephants with flower garlands, and they decorated the seats with flowers.

Everyone who attended the wedding got a silver coin. Even the king came to the wedding. He gave a gold ornament for Sita and a horse chariot for Kannan.

Musicians from all over the country came and performed for three days. The villagers had never witnessed a wedding like this. The entire village feasted, and did not feel hungry for three days after.

Rama acted as Sita's mother during *kanyadan*, a tradition where Hindu parents perform during a wedding. They give away their daughter to the groom, and from that time onward, the daughter was no longer a part of their family.

Kelu sat outside on a chair, staring out at the fading evening light, trying to relax, but his mind was far from at ease. His thoughts kept circling back to that night— the night he had taken lives to exact revenge.

The people he had killed were from a higher caste, a group who had tormented his family and others like them.

At the time, it had felt like justice, the only way to restore the balance. But the aftermath had been a constant weight on him.

Though the investigation had gone nowhere, Kelu couldn't forget how close he had come to being discovered. The authorities had searched for answers, but they found nothing substantial.

Yet, the fear remained. No one spoke of it openly, but the presence of Rama and Sita—still here, still moving quietly around the house—was a constant reminder of his past actions.

As if on cue, Sita approached, 'Thampra, I am blessed. You are my God. I would have rotted in that hell. You saved me and look at me now. I am married to your own son. Thank you for everything,'

Kelu called her to come and sit nearby him. He held her hands and looked at her. 'Take care of Kannan. He went through a lot. His father was an eminent man. He helped many people like you. More than me. You should know my—'

Kelu saw Lakshmi coming and did not finish his sentence. Instead, he said, 'Look, Lakshmi is here. She can vouch for how Vinay was.'

Lakshmi smiled. 'What are you doing here? Sita, be with Kannan. I know my husband can be very irritating. You go now and escape.'

They all laughed. Sita walked away shyly.

Lakshmi sat down with Kelu and pinched him. 'You are getting old. Still, you have the magnetic charisma to hold youthful girls around you.'

Kelu smiled and hugged her. 'Lakshmi, I am enjoying my life. You are my life. I am content. My son got married to an exquisite girl. Next, both my daughters. I am sure God will bring someone. Then it will be just us and our world.' He kissed her forehead.

Savitri walked in. She saw Kelu kissing Lakshmi and turned to leave, but hit a pot nearby.

Kelu and Lakshmi quickly turned and saw her. Lakshmi called out to her. 'Sister, come here. Don't be shy. We've known each other for many years.'

Savitri felt awkward being there. She found it very hard to look at Kelu and he felt the same way.

Lakshmi talked about how beautiful the wedding was. Savitri and Kelu did not say much.

Kelu got up and left after a few minutes to get his cart ready. Time to leave. Lakshmi noticed the awkwardness between Kelu and Savitri. Again, she wondered, *is there something going on between them?*

A few days after they returned from the wedding, Kelu brought a youthful man home with him. His name was Surya. He was very handsome and well mannered. No one knew where he was from.

Kelu was like that; if he liked someone, he would welcome him and keep him around. If he hated someone, Kelu could be their worst enemy.

People even whispered that Kelu had killed a few, but no one spoke openly against him. He was too powerful. And though he never mistreated Lakshmi, she was not happy with him. He was not the same as he was before Vinay died. She could see the changes in him, especially after his Pala trips. Still, Lakshmi never reacted.

One day, Bhavani asked, 'Mother, have you noticed whenever father goes to Pala he stays there for at least a week? He does not do that on any other trips. Maximum two days. Why is that? I don't like his behavior when he comes back from Pala either. He gets very moody for days. Is there anything wrong with the business there? I think I might go with him one day to see that business.'

'No, daughter, it is not business. Vinay's death must haunt him.'

Bhavani had many other questions, but Lakshmi avoided her by walking away to the kitchen. Lakshmi didn't know how to react here.

Kelu had given her everything and supported her family. Because of him, she had two beautiful daughters and her father and mother lived in luxury. Her sisters had married into high-caste families. Maybe the gods were punishing her a little, but she would be okay.

Lakshmi's memories went back before her marriage time. She had a friend. Her name was Laya.

She was the most beautiful, outgoing girl in her village. She is from a low caste family who does laundry. Her parents used to go to higher caste houses and get their laundry.

One day an old man from one of those higher caste saw her. He told her parents to give her as his servant. The parents knew what would happen to their daughter. They pleaded with him not to take her daughter.

Their presence always scared Laya, and she tried not to go anywhere. She told everything to Lakshmi. She wanted to take her life.

A few days passed by, and a few people came to Laya's house. They forced her out of the house. Lakshmi could see what was happening from her house. They were helpless. They beat her parents and hung them outside their house. They took Laya with them.

Lakshmi never saw Laya again. For many years, they must have tortured Laya. She was thirteen. No one heard anything about her. There are many low caste girls whose life becomes hell, just because they are beautiful.

Lakshmi remembered that many parents dressed their children as males until they got ready to marry. It was difficult.

Tears flow down Lakshmi's cheek as there is no end to it. She realizes Kelu is the reason she did not go through hell.

Lakshmi wanted her children to grow stronger than she was. She tried to give them more freedom and always encouraged them to have their own opinion. She did not want her girls to be slaves to their husbands. She always told them to stand up for their rights. Lakshmi was training them for the future.

Bhavani was becoming like a bull. She could take anyone on with her feistiness. No one could win arguing with her.

Narayani was always a girly girl. She was very sweet, but she was very naïve at the same time. She always saw well in others. Lakshmi worried about her a lot. The world had changed, and her father had also changed a lot. She needed to see that.

Bhavani, on the other hand, was brutal. She did not have compassion for others. She always had opinions, though, and she was the only one who could speak up to Kelu.

Kelu liked that. 'Watch,' he said to Lakshmi. 'One day, Bhavani will rule this town. She is my lioness.'

Now that Narayani was eighteen, Kelu and Lakshmi wanted her to get married. They both knew and agreed on one thing: the groom had to be very hands on. She could not live independently.

Kelu knew whoever they chose must be trustworthy, and he should be interested in business.

Lakshmi asked Kelu, 'How about Surya? He seems to have a smart head on his shoulder. Why don't you find out more about him?'

Kelu looked at Lakshmi in surprise. She was always quiet, but when she was serious, she came up with some amazing ideas. Kelu liked that idea.

Surya was smart. He single-handedly ran a business in many areas, turning some struggling areas into profit. Surya also didn't drink or have any destructive habits. He was very mature, and he respected his elders.

Lakshmi smiled at him, and Kelu said, 'He is a solid man. I will enquire about his background.'

The following day, he sent a message to Surya asking him to come into town. Kelu wanted to go with him to the village where he was born.

Surya was surprised to hear Kelu's wish, but he never questioned Kelu. So, they went together to Surya's village, Mangad.

Mangad was very far from Kelu's town. It was known for hardworking farmers, paddy fields, and coconut trees.

Surya's house was an old bungalow of teak wood showcasing luxury at its finest. The door had intricate carvings, the wooden floors shone, and the grand antique furniture added to the house's rich feel.

The large garden around the house was well-kept, full of vibrant flowers and lush greenery, making the place feel peaceful and serene.

Kelu was taken aback and couldn't understand why Surya had chosen to work for him when he came from such a wealthy family.

Surya's family-owned vast lands that stretched across two mountains. The sheer scale of their property left Kelu in awe.

As he took in the grandeur around him, Kelu realized that he had been quite proud of his own achievements, but compared to Surya's wealth, they seemed modest.

Yet, what struck Kelu the most was Surya's humility.

Despite his immense wealth, Surya had never flaunted his riches or acted superior. He had always been down-to-earth and sincere. Kelu admired this quality deeply.

Walking through the grand halls and the beautifully maintained gardens, Kelu couldn't help but feel a sense of respect for Surya. Here was a man who had everything yet chose to live a life of simplicity and purpose.

Kelu thought about Narayani and knew instantly that Surya was the perfect match for her. His humility, kindness, and strong sense of purpose made him the ideal partner.

Kelu met Surya's parents and was introduced to their extensive family. Surya was the eldest son, with two younger brothers and two sisters.

As they talked, Kelu noticed an odd tension in the room, particularly from Surya's father.

Surya's father finally spoke, his voice tinged with frustration.

'Surya left everything here and went to work with you as a servant. I don't understand that. He could leave you one day. He has his own mind. I warn you, he is not one you should trust with your daughter.'

Kelu was taken aback, but Surya's father continued, 'I know my son. He can detach himself from anything with minor trouble. Look at him. He is the eldest here. He knew his parents would not live long, yet he still left us and went chasing dreams. He would one day leave your daughter. Just remember that.'

These comments understandably worried Kelu. He looked at Surya. He was listening to his father, but he just smiled. Watching how he kept calm, Kelu realized that every father–son relationship could be rocky.

'Do you like Narayani?' Kelu asked Surya.

'Yes, I like her. I am not sure whether Narayani likes me. We have never talked all this time I worked for you.'

'That's all right, we will find out from her.' Kelu chuckled.

Surya's father did not like that a bit, but no reaction showed on his face. He stood like a statue.

Kelu looked at Surya's father. 'Do you have any objection to this alliance? I am not as wealthy as you, but I have a comfortable living. I will share half of my wealth with Narayani.'

'I am not worried about your wealth, Kelu. I am worried about your daughter. It seems to me, however, that perhaps Surya has changed. He has kept his job with you for many years. So, I will try to think positive here. As a father, though, it was my duty to caution you. I know my son very well. He has always been immature and opportunistic.'

Kelu and Surya stayed that night at Surya's bungalow. Kelu did not sleep well. He was happy and nervous at the same time. He wished Lakshmi was with him. She had a good sense of these things. He tossed and turned, the thoughts piling up.

Am I making the right decision?

Is Surya going to take care of my daughter?

Narayani has no mean bone in her. She is so fragile. I cannot see her suffer.

Kelu got up and went to Surya's room. He pulled him out of his bed.

'You better take care of her, otherwise you will see my mean side. My daughter is precious to me, but she is naïve. Surya, you better be true to what you have portrayed in front of me.'

The next morning, Kelu got up and got ready. Surya did the same. As they climbed into the bullock cart, Surya's father came out and gave them food for the journey back. While they traveled, they did not talk to each other. Both were deep in thought.

Surya realized he'd never really seen Narayani. He'd caught glimpses here and there, but he wanted to get back and see her properly.

He looked at Kelu, who seemed to be very serious. He was hitting hard at the bullocks.

He wanted the cart to move faster, even though the bullocks were already running as fast as they could.

The sun settled down after its efforts to keep Earth warm, the orange light painting the clouds. Surya gazed at the clouds, and his heart was filled with joy. He saw the world differently. He felt the air had a fresh aroma to it. He felt a sweetness in everything he saw. *Was this the feeling of falling in love?*

He looked at Kelu, and even Kelu seemed attractive to him. Surya floated around in deep thought.

The cart hit a deep pothole, jolting Kelu and Surya back to reality. They realized they'd traveled the entire day without stopping.

The bullocks were exhausted, and they knew they'd pushed the animals too hard. They stopped and took the load off the bullocks' backs and let them graze and drink. Kelu and Surya both ate. Still, no one talked.

Finally, Surya gathered some courage and broke the silence. 'I will take care of your daughter. Do not worry. Still, we need to find out whether she has the same feelings for me.'

Kelu smiled at Surya and patted his back. 'I know you will, son.'

It was the first time Kelu had called him son. It felt good.

They got the bullocks back to the cart. There was fresh energy in both of them, re-energized and ready to finish the journey back home.

Kelu usually dropped Surya at the staff quarters where all his servants slept. That evening, he took Surya to his outbuilding. Kelu usually only provided outbuilding to relatives. The cart stopped in front of the outhouse. Surya did not move a bit. Surya looked at him in surprise. Kelu told him, 'Today onward, you stay here till things get sorted out.'

Kelu pushed him out of the cart and rode away.

In the main house, Lakshmi was patiently waiting for Kelu's return.

'And?' she asked Kelu when he walked in.

'The family is wonderful and well settled, but...'

'But what?'

'His father was not sure about Surya. He said we cannot trust Surya, that he likes to move from place to place. He said Surya is an opportunistic person.'

'What you think?'

'What I think doesn't matter. First, we have to find out what's on Narayani's mind.'

'I talked to her after you went. She likes him.'

'That makes it harder, doesn't it? I was hoping she would say no to this alliance. As a father, I am scared to make this decision.'

'I think he is good. I have that feeling. He will be good for Narayani.'

Kelu looked at Lakshmi for a while, then abruptly said, 'Let's do it. At least we know him. Better than a stranger. We just need to keep him occupied and watch him closely.'

'It's their life. I don't want you to spy on him. I know you; you will not give them any freedom.'

Kelu smiled and sat by her. He held her hands and said, 'You don't know how a father feels. His responsibility is higher than anyone's for his daughter. Mother carries them in their womb for nine months, but a father carries them in their hearts for a lifetime. The responsibility of making sure daughters are safe after marriage is heavy, dear. I am worried about Narayani. She is so naïve. I will kill him if he makes her cry.'

They both laughed at Kelu's ferocious speech.

Narayani and Bhavani walked in. They hadn't seen their parents laughing like this for a long time. The girls giggled and Kelu and Lakshmi quickly separated from their hug. They looked at their daughters. Both were so beautiful.

Narayani always kept her hair braided and dressed elegantly. Bhavani was more the tomboyish type. They loved each other deeply. Bhavani, though younger than Narayani, kept her sister from danger. She ruled the house.

Bhavani asked, 'What is there to laugh about this much, parents? Share with us.'

'We found a man for Narayani. He will come tomorrow to see her.'

Bhavani spoke her mind. 'You cannot do this. You should ask her before you bring some guy here.'

Narayani pinched her hard.

'What, you agree with them? They can bring whoever they want and you will marry them? Not in my house. I won't let that happen. Who is this guy?'

Kelu smiled while Bhavani was talking. He could see himself in her. However, the way she was behaving upset Lakshmi. She almost got up to slap her, but Kelu held her back. He wanted to see Bhavani standing up for her sister.

'It's Surya.'

'That servant!? You couldn't find anyone else? Narayani, let me tell you something. You can find someone better. Father wants a slave who will listen to him. Don't agree to this.'

Narayani did not speak, only looked down shyly.

Bhavani pulled her sister and walked away, saying, 'Let me put some sense into you. Idiot.'

Kelu laughed so hard he nearly fell over. Lakshmi was mad, but seeing her husband happy, she also smiled.

'See, Bhavani is just like me. I am sure she will take care of the family and the business after my death. I got a lioness in her.'

Lakshmi put her head on to his chest. She took a long breath, as if she was releasing all her tension. Kelu held her tight, and they fell asleep like that.

The following day, Bhavani was still not happy. She wanted Narayani to tell their father she didn't want this marriage.

But Narayani liked Surya. She had no unpleasant feelings about him, and he was good-looking and had a superb physique. He was also hardworking. She didn't understand why Bhavani was this upset.

She told her, 'I am okay with Father's decision. I want to be an obedient daughter, and I am sure he would not make grim decisions.'

Bhavani was furious. She walked out, slamming the door.

Bhavani went to Kelu's office. 'Father, I am not happy. I want to talk to Surya before you bring him here. You don't know Narayani like I do. I want to make sure this is the right guy.'

'That is not the culture. You cannot talk to him.'

'I am not asking what the culture is. I want to talk to him, period. If not, I will die. You can have this wedding after you are done with my funeral.'

Kelu stopped writing. He got up. Bhavani sensed his anger and moved back. Kelu came forward and grabbed her hand. He pulled her out of the door. She had to run to keep up with him.

He threw her in the bullock cart and started riding. Bhavani got scared. She wanted to call out for her mother, but it was already too late. She kept quiet. Kelu was her father. He would not bring harm to her. The cart stopped in front of an outbuilding.

'So, are you going to keep me here till this wedding is over? Father, I could still fight and you know that. You cannot keep me as a prisoner.'

Bhavani screamed as loud as she could. Kelu slapped her. It was the first time he'd ever done that, and it shocked her.

'You wanted to talk to Surya. Go talk now. He is inside. But don't you dare ever talk to me like this again. I am your father. I made you, and I could destroy you too. Never take this kind of attitude with me again, ever. I am doing this because I know you want the best for your sister. So do what you have to do with Surya. I will wait outside.'

Bhavani couldn't believe what just happened. It drained her. She now knew why people said Kelu can be brutal. She'd just seen the fire in him.

She did not know what to say to Surya. Then again, she felt the need to help her sister, so she walked to the door and knocked. She waited, but no one answered. She pushed the door a little, and it opened.

Bhavani entered. 'Surya, where are you?'

Just then, Surya walked out of the bathroom. He was naked. Bhavani screamed, as he did also. He quickly put a towel around his waist.

'Aren't you ashamed to walk naked in the house?'

'You are the one who walked in without announcing yourself.'

'Are you deaf? I called your name.'

'I was bathing so did not hear you calling. Sorry.'

Bhavani had a smile on her face. Her anger melted a little now that she'd seen him at his most vulnerable.

She couldn't deny that he was good-looking, also well built. He was an excellent fit for her sister.

'Put some clothes on and come out,' she told him. 'I need to talk to you.' She went out, giggling.

Surya was in shock with embarrassment. He quickly got ready and went to the verandah. He could see Kelu waiting outside by the cart. He sensed something was not right. Bhavani was standing with her back to the door.

He stood behind her and said, 'I am here. What do you want to talk about?'

'Why do you want to marry my sister?'

'Well, your father asked me.'

'So, you don't truly want to marry? You are marrying because my father asked?'

'It's not like that.'

'Then what?'

'I want to marry her. I like her.'

'Liking her and wanting to marry her are different. I want to know why you want to marry her. Just liking her is not enough. Look, she's very naïve. I will not tolerate it if you ruin her life.'

'I am not a bad person. I will take care of her. I don't need your father's money. I will work hard and make sure I give her an excellent life. I don't know how to say more. Is that good enough for you?'

'Well, I will think about it. You look good naked. I will tell this to my sister.' She ran off giggling. Surya felt his skin burning with embarrassment.

Kelu saw Bhavani coming toward the cart giggling. He felt good. As soon as their eyes met, Bhavani tried to keep her face serious, but Kelu started laughing.

'So. Do you approve this marriage, Thampratti?'

'I saw him naked.' She laughed again.

Kelu couldn't say anything to that. It puzzled him though. Why naked? Oh god. He hoped she hadn't asked him to strip down. Was that why she came all the way here? It can't be.

'Well, it's up to Narayani now. I don't care,' she said.

They both laughed.

Kelu said, 'Naked. My God. He must be half dead from embarrassment by now. It wounds his pride for sure.'

He steered the bullock cart away from the outbuilding premises.

Lakshmi saw Kelu and Bhavani walking in.

'You both look happy today,' she said. 'I cannot remember the last time I saw you both like this without arguments. What happened?'

'Narayani is getting married to Surya,' Kelu said, so loud that everyone in the house could hear. 'Let's get ready for a wedding!'

They all hugged. Still, Bhavani had reservations about Surya. She would keep a close watch on him. She wanted her sister to be happy.

***

Part Four: Narayani

Lakshmi wanted Narayani's wedding done right. Narayani would say nothing, and Kelu would not ask either, so Lakshmi felt she needed to stand up for her daughter. She invited the whole village.

Savitri, Kannan, Sita and Rama arrived one week early. Every time Savitri was around, Kelu acted strange. He did not talk much, and he stayed away from the house and worked more.

Lakshmi and Bhavani kept busy arranging decorations, food and ornaments for Narayani.

Kelu invited the king to the wedding. This time, the king sent his personal dance performers from the palace to entertain the guests.

Surya's parents and siblings came and stayed in the outbuilding. Kelu made sure all their needs were taken care of with no delays.

Kannan did everything as Narayani's older brother. He took care of all the outside work, including decorations around the house.

Three days before the marriage, the whole village had its roads lit by oil lamps. Every evening, they had fireworks and dance programs. They also treated everyone who came over with amazing food. Kelu brought in fresh arrack so everyone could get drunk.

Bhavani never dressed like a girl, but Lakshmi forced her to wear ornaments and dress properly. With hesitation, she did.

The villagers had never seen her beauty like this. They told Kelu how beautiful Bhavani was, filling him with pride.

On the wedding day, twelve elephants were in front of the house. They welcomed Surya and his family. Surya looked like a prince in his white attire and wore grand headgear. Elephants adorned him with a garland, while other elephants sprinkled rose water on everyone who came with Surya.

Kannan and Kelu came out. Kannan washed Surya's feet, and then hugged him.

'Surya, welcome. Narayani is beautiful inside and out, with not a mean bone in her. You are a lucky man for sure. But you are also very unlucky.'

Surya looked at Kannan, puzzled, and stepped back from the hug. With a smile, Kannan stood beside him and they both walked toward the marriage altar.

'You are unlucky because she has a brother like me and a sister like Bhavani. We will slice you into many pieces if you become a reason for Narayani to cry.'

Surya stopped walking. Kannan turned and welcomed him one more time, then walked away.

They had decorated the altar with red roses. On one side, there was a tall oil lamp. In the middle, they had nice low seats.

In front of the seats, the priest sat by the fire, ready for prayer. He was waiting for Surya to walk in and take his place.

Surya was not at all happy with Kannan's comments. Suddenly, he felt a hold on his hand. Startled, he looked and saw that his father pulled Surya toward the altar.

He realized the ceremony had started. His father led him around the fire three times and asked him to sit. Music played and the bride came out of the house. Everyone gasped.

Narayani was like a goddess. Her red saree and ornaments were stunning. People had never seen such a beauty before. Surya stared at her and forgot about his worries.

Then he saw Kannan and Bhavani walking with Narayani. Surya tried to keep his composure and smiled.

Halfway to the altar, Kelu joined Narayani and led her the rest of the way. Narayani sat on Kelu's lap for *kanyadan* ceremony.

Kelu had tears in his eyes and Lakshmi openly cried with joy.

Bhavani's heart raced, but Kannan assured her everything would be okay.

Narayani was happy. She felt that Surya was the best thing that ever happened to her. Usually, after marriage, the bride goes to the husband's house.

But as Surya was always working with her father, Narayani never really had to leave her own house.

Surya played a major role in Kelu's business, and Kelu started trusting Surya more and more. He sometimes saw Vinay in him. His ability to forecast and his business acumen always surprised him.

Surya became hungrier about making money. Kelu told him to take it slow, but the flow of money coming in made Surya obsessed with work.

Narayani saw changes happening in him. He was more detached from home. He traveled more and didn't come home every week. Sometimes, he would go for months.

Slowly, Kelu lost his authority over him. Surya became more influenced by his recent friends. He also had his own business other than textile.

Bhavani expressed her concerns to Lakshmi, but Lakshmi always told her to keep quiet. 'If Narayani has no complaints, why are you worried? If there was any issue, I am sure Narayani would tell us.'

Bhavani doubted Narayani was capable of expressing her problems. She went to Narayani's room to confront her directly.

'Sister, are you happy?'

'Of course I am happy. Why do you ask?'

'I can see what's happening here. You've been married almost two years, and I've seen brother-in-law only four times in this house the last year.'

'Well, he is taking care of our father's business. He's bringing us wealth. Don't you dare question me like this, Bhavani.'

Narayani tried to be strong, but she couldn't. She burst into tears and fell onto Bhavani's shoulder. 'Sister, I am helpless. He was not like before. He rarely comes to our house. He doesn't love me anymore. I don't want Father to feel bad. He exalts him.'

Bhavani seethed with anger. She pulled away from her sister and started to leave.

'Please don't make a scene,' Narayani begged her. 'I will live like this. He's not harming me. I am happy the way it is.'

Bhavani turned around and slapped Narayani. 'I am ashamed to call you my sister. You cannot live like this as a slave. I will not let this happen. I will kill him.'

Lakshmi heard Bhavani's raised voice and rushed to Narayani's room. She saw Narayani crying and holding Bhavani's feet.

'Narayani, what are you doing? You are the elder sister. You should never beg your younger sister.'

Bhavani looked at her mother, her eyes glowing with anger.

Lakshmi knew something was very wrong. She stood in front of Bhavani and said, 'You are my daughter, and I have the same hot blood like you. Don't you dare move out of this room without telling me what has happened and what you plan to do?'

Bhavani realized then it was her mother's feistiness she had inherited, not her father's. She had a sense of pride about that.

Bhavani told everything to her mother. Narayani kept weeping. She did not have the courage to talk.

'Narayani, this is your life,' Lakshmi said. 'You need to get up from this self-pity and start defending yourself. I cannot believe all this has happened. Neither your father nor I knew about it. I knew he was not coming home that often, but I thought he loved you when he was here. This is not at all acceptable. I cannot think of a time when your father went for months and came back cold-hearted like Surya is.'

'That is not true, Mother,' Bhavani said. 'I have seen Father behaving badly when he comes back from Pala. I know it, and you know it. I hate men dictating women's lives here. Look, whether or not you support me, I will fight for my sister's happiness. Or else I will kill him while doing that.'

There was a long moment of uncomfortable silence, then they heard Kelu's laughing voice approaching outside. Kelu walked in with Surya.

'Look who is here, my son, Surya. He won a major contract with one of the biggest exporters of linen to six major provinces.'

'So what?' Bhavani said. 'He cannot even take care of his own house, but he wants to do business.' She stared at Surya and said, 'You do not know me that well, but I will ruin you.'

Kelu couldn't even react before Surya slapped Bhavani's face. No one moved. No one had ever dared do something like that in front of Kelu.

It seemed as though even nature paused, as if the trees, flowers, and wind had all felt the strike.

Narayani fainted and fell backward, striking her head on the floor. She couldn't handle the immense emotional pressure.

Lakshmi saw how the atmosphere had changed. She knew what just happened would turn into a storm.

Kelu moved forward, but Surya grabbed his neck and said, 'Old man, don't you dare. I've had enough of you and your daughter ruling my daily life. I am taking over here. If you want to live under my roof, then obey. Otherwise, you can all leave right now.'

'Surya, I have treated you as my own child. Don't forget, I can take back all you have, your job and your business. Everything around you is mine. You are married to my daughter so I am giving some respect, otherwise, your head and your hand would both roll.'

Surya laughed. 'The papers I've had you sign all these months? They were property and business transfer documents. You have nothing, Kelu. Nothing. Whatever I give you, take it and live here without complaint.'

Surya walked out.

Kelu looked at Lakshmi, helpless.

Lakshmi smiled weakly at Kelu and said, 'God will be with us. Don't you worry.'

Kelu broke down and started to cry. No one had ever seen him this defeated.

'No!' Bhavani said. 'No one cries here. We will fight back. This is not something we should accept. I will kill him, for you and for Narayani.'

As she said that, they realized Narayani was still lying on the floor, not moving. They picked her up and took her to bed.

Bhavani put some water on her face and called her name. Still, Narayani did not move. Bhavani looked to her father, but he was useless now. She ran out and readied the bullock cart, intending to get help.

Surya stopped her. 'If you want to take this cart, you need permission from me. Go inside.'

Bhavani jumped down from the cart and kicked him hard.

Surya had not expected that and he fell backward. She took the cart and ran over his leg. Surya screamed with pain.

She yelled out, 'Your wife is not responding. Help if you are a man. I will get the *vaidyar*.' (Local herbal doctor)

Surya got up and limped inside.

Kelu confronted him. 'What did I do to you? Why did you ruin my family?'

Surya ignored him and walked to the bedside. He looked at Narayani and said, 'I am glad that you are vegetable now. I wanted money, a big house, and fame. I couldn't do this to my own father, so I saw your father as an opportunity. I am king now.'

Lakshmi walked over to Surya and spat in his face. She cursed him. 'All this you have gained will not give you peace. You will die alone in pain that is my wish.'

Surya slapped Lakshmi.

Kelu charged his back and tried to put him in a headlock. But Surya was young and strong, and he pushed Kelu down.

Surya pulled Lakshmi to another room and locked her in. He said, 'From today, you will live in that room. If you behave, you will get food. Otherwise, you can rot in there.'

Kelu rose to his knees and folded his hands. He begged Surya to spare his wife and kids. 'Leave us alone. We will go to Pala and live there. You can have all this.'

'No, you will live here with me. I want the villagers to think I am the best thing that has happened to this family. I want pride and fame. Money I would make regardless.'

He laughed and walked out, limping.

'Where is Mother?' Bhavani asked Kelu, her voice cracking under the strain.

Kelu pointed toward a locked door at the far end of the house. The silence was oppressive, and Bhavani's dread grew thicker by the second.

Without a word, she sprinted outside, grabbed a sledgehammer from the storage shed, and returned with it, her resolve hardening with each step.

The sound of the door shattering under her blows echoed through the house, each hit a desperate attempt to break through the suffocating tension. When the door finally gave way, Bhavani rushed inside.

The sight that greeted her was a nightmare. Lakshmi, her mother, was hanging from a beam in the roof. The room was filled with an eerie stillness, and Bhavani's heart nearly stopped.

This wasn't the woman she remembered—Lakshmi, who had once fought fiercely for her family, who had taken lives to protect them. The strong, determined mother who had always been a pillar of strength.

Kelu followed, his face contorted with shock. He collapsed to his knees, his breath coming in ragged gasps as he stared at Lakshmi's lifeless body.

The disbelief and guilt were overwhelming. He had been so wrapped up in his own world, in the danger and secrets of his life in Pala, that he hadn't noticed the growing despair in Lakshmi. The woman who had stood by him, who had carried the weight of their family's struggles, was gone.

Tears streamed down Kelu's face as he reached out helplessly. He should have seen the signs. He should have been more present. His mind raced with a torrent of regrets and the crushing realization that he had failed her. The pressure from every side, the weight of his own actions and the constant reminders of his past, had been too much for her.

Bhavani, still holding the sledgehammer, stood in the doorway, her hands trembling. She had come seeking help, only to find her mother dead. The gravity of the situation was sinking in, and she felt a profound sense of loss and helplessness.

The room was filled with a heavy silence, the weight of Lakshmi's death pressing down on everyone. Suicide seemed inconceivable for someone like her. The air was thick with sorrow and disbelief, and the once strong and resolute family seemed shattered.

Kelu's heart torn apart by the devastating sight of Lakshmi's lifeless body hanging from the beam. His mind raced with a whirlwind of emotions, each more agonizing than the last. He couldn't shake the memories of their journey together—the battles they had fought to be together against all odds, the dreams they had shared of a future filled with happiness and love.

He had believed their love was unbreakable, a bond that would weather any storm. Yet, now, faced with the harsh reality of her sudden departure, he felt an overwhelming sense of betrayal mixed with profound sadness.

His heart ached with regret and longing, wishing he could turn back time and rewrite their story. Anger simmered beneath the surface, directed at himself for not being able to protect her, and at the circumstances that had driven her to such a desperate act.

He clenched his fists, feeling powerless against the tidal wave of emotions crashing over him. Tears welled up in his eyes, his throat tight with unspoken words and unspeakable sorrow.

'You coward! I am ashamed to be your daughter,' Bhavani screamed, breaking the silence. Her voice was filled with a mix of anger and heartbreak. 'I never thought you would run away from troubles like this. Go to hell. I will face this.'

She turned to Kelu. 'Anyone else who wants to run away, now is the time. I will stay here and fight till my last breath.'

The vaidyar approached Bhavani.

'Is she okay?'

'No. I am afraid she is no longer with us.'

Bhavani was shocked into silence. She looked at Lord Krishna's picture and prayed. *Why, Lord? Why this much punishment? Why take my mother and sister? They are innocent. They only loved others. Why them? You could have taken my father or me. This is cruel. Do you think I will break down? No, Lord. I will fight. I will not let Surya ruin my family. This is a promise.*

Bhavani sat down and stared at the floor. Her mind was furious. She knew she needed to change her approach. This anger and fighting Surya out in the open would not work.

She realized she needed to trap him the same way he had trapped her father.

Sitting there, she did not know how much time had passed, but the sun went down, and it turned dark.

She heard Surya crying outside. She walked out and saw Surya sitting and crying in front of the villagers.

He noticed her and asked her to stand by his side. He hugged her and continued crying.

'Why, Bhavani, why? Your sister has left us. Our mother too. This has devastated poor Kelu, rendered him useless. What happened? I am very unlucky. My parents don't want me, now my wife and her mother have left me too. I have a cursed life.'

He turned to Bhavani with a small smirk on his face, then leaned forward and hugged her again.

This time, Bhavani pushed him away. 'Surya, don't you worry. I will take care of you. I will be your family.'

The village leader came forward. 'Bhavani, your father is helpless now. You should run the business from now onward. Surya will help you. You are a brave girl, and we will support you if you need anything. We respect your father and we have seen how capable you are.'

He turned to Surya. 'Today onward, Bhavani will replace Kelu. We want you to support her in all needs.'

Surya couldn't say much other than to accept it. He could not say he had the business now. If he did, everyone would have doubts about his wife's and mother-in-law's deaths.

Bhavani realized now Surya could not act like they owned the business, at least not in front of the villagers. That had bought her some time to plan.

Bhavani's hands trembled as she reached for her mother's lifeless form. The once strong, vibrant Lakshmi was gone, taken by the weight of her own struggles.

The grief was a physical force, pressing down on her chest, making it hard to breathe. She felt an emptiness so profound that it threatened to consume her whole.

Kelu, kneeling beside Lakshmi, was also overcome by the depth of his sorrow. His face was streaked with tears, his hands clutching at his hair as if trying to grasp reality itself.

His heart ached with the knowledge that he had not only failed his wife but had also been blind to the pain of his daughter Narayani.

The loss of Narayani had been unbearable, but seeing Lakshmi in this state was a pain he hadn't anticipated. He felt as though he was drowning in his own failures, his emotions a tangled mess of regret and despair.

Kelu's sobs filled the room, raw and uncontrollable. He remembered Narayani's laugh, her warmth, the way she had tried to hold the family together despite the chaos. And now, to see her mother gone too, felt like an unbearable weight pressing down on him.

He had been so consumed by his own fears and needs that he had neglected to notice the crumbling world around him.

Bhavani sank to her knees beside Lakshmi, her tears falling onto the cold floor. She reached out for her mother's hand, gripping it tightly as if hoping for some last sign of connection. Her sobs were deep, wrenching, each breathe a struggle against the crushing reality of their loss.

Kelu, seeing Bhavani's anguish, reached out to her, pulling her into a tight embrace. They wept together, their tears mingling, their shared grief a bond that neither of them could have prepared for.

The loss of both Narayani and Lakshmi was a blow that left them both hollow, their hearts broken by the enormity of their sorrow.

As they clung to each other, the house seemed to close in around them, the walls echoing with the sounds of their despair.

The once vibrant home was now a place of mourning, the loss of their loved ones casting a long shadow over their lives. The weight of their grief was all-consuming, a reminder of the fragility of their happiness and the heavy cost of the lives they had led.

Late that night, they cremated Narayani and Lakshmi. Women rarely go to the cremation ceremony. Kelu, however, would not get up from where he was sitting. He sat there half dead.

Bhavani decided not to let Surya do the cremation. She fought with the villagers. The village leader tried to make her understand that only men could do this ceremony. Bhavani ignored them.

'I am the rightful person to cremate them. I am her daughter and her sister. I have to do this. I do not care about this rule. I will go to hell if this does not please the gods, but I am sure my sister and my mother will go to heaven, regardless.'

Surya tried to stop her from going to the cremation.

Bhavani turned on him and he saw the fire in her. 'You dare Surya, and you will pay the price right now.' She pushed him aside. Surya did not move much, but he let her go.

Bhavani walked to the side of the well. She took her sari out and asked Surya to bring her a dhoti, a long cloth piece worn in South India around your body in the form of a skirt. She tied the dhoti from her chest down.

Usually, only men do this ritual, which includes taking a bath. She did the same. She took her undergarments off, and the villagers cried even more when they saw her doing this. Surya stood still. All this time, Bhavani stared at him.

She drew a bucket of water from the well and poured the water on herself. The dhoti stuck to her body. She was crying, but no one noticed as she was wet.

She walked toward the ceremony place. There, she saw two pyres ready with her mother and sister. People started crying louder when they saw Bhavani dressed for the ceremony.

She told everyone to stop crying. She wanted her mother's and sister's last moments to be peaceful and silent. She walked around the pyres three times with a pot of water on her head.

Each time she got to their heads, the priest would break a little on the pot and let the water flow. Every time she reached their heads, she promised them she would take revenge on Surya.

She was getting stronger and stronger mentally. The third time, she dropped the pot down by their heads.

The priest gave her the fire stick and asked her to light the pyres. She did, with no hesitation. She was smiling inside.

A new Bhavani was being born as the fire raged through the bodies, like a phoenix rising from the ashes. She turned and smiled at Surya, who felt a bit of a shiver through his spine. He saw the goddess Durga in front of the fire.

She walked toward Surya, went very close to him, held his hand and said, 'Thank you, Surya for doing this. I wanted to do this a long time ago. I am sick and tired of living this so-called straight life. This is amazing.'

She pinched his stomach and pulled his hand toward her inner thigh, then walked away quickly before he could say anything or react.

Bhavani hurried back toward home. She could feel the heat from the fire on her back. She felt like she was burning inside. She was crying while walking, and not sure where she was heading from here.

She only knew one thing. She would make Surya's life miserable. She would break him down and make him live under her feet. She had that determination. She looked back and saw Surya still standing there, looking at her. She felt that she was winning already.

Many villagers were standing in front of the house. Bhavani asked them to leave, saying she wanted some space for herself. They got up and left, crying as they were leaving. Bhavani saw Kelu still sitting in the same corner with his head down. She went to him.

'Father, I can do this. I will get back everything we lost today. I am sorry that I was not there to protect our family. I was blind. I want your blessing and support.'

Kelu looked up. 'Bhavani, I never saw this coming. I thought I was doing everything right. I should have taken your advice and not let Surya enter our family. Now, I have lost everything. My love, Lakshmi. I lost her. I cannot live without her. She was everything for me. She was the pillar behind my success. I broke her heart. How could I do this?'

Bhavani pulled Kelu up and shook him. 'Look, you made all this by your hard work. You made me. I will be your strength. All I want from you is not to doubt me from now on. I will move through various paths, whether right or wrong, my only goal being to bring Surya down. I will do that, Father. I will. Now stop crying, play along, and do as I say.'

She pulled him inside a room and closed the door. A few hours later, Bhavani came out.

The pyres were still burning and people were still around the fire. Surya had to stay until it was all burned. Bhavani stood in the doorway as the night breeze slowly started.

Chilly wind touched her. She stood and watched the pyres go down until they were just hot coals. She saw a familiar figure walking toward her. Surya.

She pulled Kelu outside and shouted at him. 'You ruined this family. I don't want to see you here again.' Bhavani pushed Kelu off the verandah and told Surya, 'Here, I am done with him.'

Surya grabbed Kelu by his neck.

'Surya, don't touch him. Keep him in the outbuilding. We will tell the villagers he is sick.'

Surya thought that was an outstanding idea. He walked with Kelu to the outbuilding.

Bhavani couldn't believe Surya was not questioning her, or even doubting her.

She walked in the house with tears flowing down her cheeks, but kept her composure.

There were three maids there. They looked at her in awe, seeing the change in her.

Bhavani went close to them and said, 'Do you trust me?'

'Yes, Thampratti, we trust you.'

'Okay. Then you act as if nothing is happening here. Time will tell you why I am doing this. Trust me.'

**

Part 5: Kannan

Bhavani went to her room. She closed the door, fell down on the bed and cried herself to sleep. She woke the following morning to lots of noise outside. She peeped out to see what was happening and saw Surya with a few people talking outside by the verandah.

One of the people was the village leader. Bhavani quickly pulled her hair up and adjusted her clothes, then walked out to the verandah.

The village leader approached Bhavani. 'What happened to Kelu? Surya is saying he is not talking anymore and doesn't want to see anyone.'

Bhavani felt a shock through her spine. She looked at Surya, who smiled and winked at her.

She said, 'Father is in shock now. He will come out in a few days for sure. Right now, he doesn't want to see anybody but family. I will see him today and make sure he is okay. Everyone is just tired.'

The village leader held her hand and moved forward to whisper in her ear. 'We have heard many dreadful things about Surya. I am not so sure about him being here. Do you want us to tell him to go back to his hometown? We could help you run the business. You are like our daughter, and your father was like our brother.'

She held his hand tight. 'Don't worry, I will manage. If I need help, I will definitely accept your generous offer.'

Everyone offered their condolences again, then left.

Bhavani walked toward the kitchen and Surya followed her. She could sense his weakness. She walked slower and let him watch her, then stopped so quickly that Surya walked into her.

She gave him a quick smile, then ran off to the kitchen. Bhavani asked the maid who was there to stay.

Surya walked in, saw the maid there, asked for a glass of water, and then quickly left.

Bhavani glanced at the maid, who had a smirk on her face. Neither said a word. Bhavani sat down by the door, suddenly overcome with sorrow. Since yesterday, she had just been reacting to situations, thinking a mile a minute.

She needed to pause a little and properly grieve her loss. The maid sat down by her and Bhavani laid her head on the maid's lap. They sat like that for a long time, the silence and companionship giving them peace.

Surya went to the outbuilding where Kelu was locked in. Upon entering, he could tell Kelu had not slept. His eyes were red, like hot fire coals.

Kelu knew Surya was there to say something, but he did not get up from the bed. Surya came closer and said, 'Look, old man, I will marry Bhavani. I am not asking you, but telling you. All you have to do is come and bless our marriage. Tell you the truth, she is much better than your first one.'

Kelu got up from the bed in anger. 'In your dreams she will marry you.'

'Bhavani has already asked me to marry her. I thought I would tell you so you could rot here thinking about it. I think she has lost her mind, but I don't care. I will use her.'

Kelu laughed. 'I think you are the one who has lost your mind.'

Surya slapped him. 'What is there to laugh at, you idiot? I'll show you how this entire land will come to be mine without even lifting a finger.'

Kelu looked at Surya in dismay. How could a person change so quickly? He turned his back as Surya left and walked to the window.

Sun was shining on the dewdrops, and a light breeze fluttered past. It was a beautiful morning. Kelu sat down by the window and cried.

Surya approached the verandah and saw Bhavani heading his way, toward the outbuilding.

'Why do you need to go there? I am here to take care of the old man.' Surya thought he saw a flash of anger in her eyes, but Bhavani quickly changed her approach. She took his hand and placed it over her heart.

'I know you will take care of him, but I want to do it myself. I am sick and tired of living under him and my older sister. You know I am the smartest, yet I have always had to listen to him. He liked her more than me.'

'So, this is my chance to take care of him. You know, really take care of him.'

She winked at him with a devious smile.

Surya couldn't hear a word she was saying. All he could focus on was feeling his hand on her chest. He went closer to her.

Bhavani felt a flash of anger, but she stayed still as Surya hugged her. She had her hand on the dagger she always kept in her underskirt. She began to pull it, but then Surya moved away from her. She smiled at him, then walked past him toward the outbuilding.

Surya started to follow her.

'No, you don't come with me. I am not so cruel as to ridicule him in front of others. I want to make him feel little only in front of me. You go now and I will meet you at the house. Let me show you what I am really made of.'

Surya was excited by her words and hastened back to the main house.

Bhavani entered the outbuilding and saw her father sitting by the window and crying. She ran to him and fell at his feet.

'Father, forgive me. I had no choice but to act like this. Trust me, I will regain what we lost yesterday. Please do not give up on me.'

Kelu kicked her away. 'Move, you idiot. I heard about your plan to marry that rascal. He came here and told me the happy news.'

Bhavani fell backward, then regained her balance. She sat by the wall near the door and did not say anything for a long time.

Finally, she said, 'Father, I cannot fight against him without bringing him closer to me. I know what I am doing. You need to trust me. I will ruin him with a painfully slow process. He will not get up from this. I'll make sure of that.'

Kelu smiled ruefully. 'Yes, a painfully slow process. You don't know him. He will destroy you, just like he did with me, your mother and sister. I do not want to lose you. Please don't marry him. We can just leave here and move to Pala. Kannan will take care of us. Why should we stay here and deal with this devil?'

'I am not moving away from my home. Can't you see Mother and Narayani are here? They will not forgive us if we run away. I promised them when I did the pyre that I would kill Surya. I am not backing out from my plan.'

'Okay then, smart girl, what's your plan?' he asked sarcastically.

Bhavani got up. 'I am ashamed to call you my father. When did you ever run away from anything? I have never seen you this defeated before. Either you support me or live like this. But you are not going away from here. I will take care of you until my last breath. I want you to die here, on your own soil. Father, you need to work with me.'

She hugged him and they both cried.

'You are my youngest daughter. I don't want you to suffer even a little, dear. I am not feeling like myself. I ruined you all because I was blinded by pride and arrogance. I should have listened to you. He was not the right one, and my family has suffered for my bad judgment. My Lakshmi was a gem. She should have lived long to see her grandchildren. My love, I am sure she would never commit suicide, but I think Surya killed her inside. Bhavani, I know you want revenge. But I have only you. Please be careful. My life is almost over anyway, but you have an entire life in front of you. Do nothing without thinking, daughter. I love you, and I trust you.'

Kelu was overcome with emotion and slumped down to the floor.

Bhavani had never seen him this weak. She always remembered her father as a person with a fire inside to fight. Now, he was not even a shadow of what he once was. She feared losing him soon.

'Father, please take care of yourself. You know me. I will see this end with no danger.'

She sat by him and hugged him. Kelu slowly fell asleep on her shoulder. Bhavani stayed with him as tears flowed down her cheeks.

After a while, Kelu woke up, confused. Bhavani led him to bed. 'Father, I will send you food. Eat nothing unless it is from my girl. Don't trust anyone here. I must leave now.'

Surya was outside the main house, waiting for Bhavani. 'Why did it take this long? I don't think you should spend that much time there. I could not wait to see you.'

Bhavani smiled and continued into the house. She asked the girl to take some food over to the outbuilding.

Surya followed Bhavani everywhere. The girl left with the food and Surya came closer to Bhavani. He looked at her and pulled her chin up. Using his index finger, he brushed the hair from her forehead.

She did not move or look at him. Her heart raced and inside she was burning with anger. He caressed her eyebrows and jawline. She moved her face to the side and tears flowed on her cheeks.

He stopped his finger by her lips and said, 'Why are you crying? I thought you were happy with this.' Bhavani said nothing. She tried to move away from him.

He held her hand and said, 'Don't worry, I will leave you alone. I know it is not time yet. I will let you process your grief. Tomorrow, I am going to Pala. I think we need to take that business back from Kannan. What do you think?'

She was excited by the news Surya would travel. She did not fancy him taking over Kannan's business.

However, she said, 'It's a brilliant decision, but we need to wait. We cannot do anything drastic too soon or people will suspect us. Surya, we need to act wisely.

Yes, go to Pala and see how things are. Stay there for a week and then come back. I will take care here. Don't you worry.'

Surya agreed with her reasoning, kissed her hand, and then went to his room.

Bhavani went outside looking for Nanamma. She walked around the house and found her near the shed for cows.

Nanamma took pride in looking after the cows. Seeing Bhavani approaching, Nanamma took her towel away from her chest, as low caste were not supposed to go about covered.

Bhavani stopped her from removing the towel. 'Nanamma, never do that anymore. My mother never believed in that, neither did my father. I am following their belief.'

'I thought you were the mean one. I know what happened inside. I cannot believe that you could put your father in the outbuilding like that. I saw everything from here in the dark yesterday. Your mother will never come to peace up there now.' She cried.

'Nanamma, I am here to ask for your help. I want revenge. I cannot let my mother and sister die in vain. I will always take care of my father.'

'Thampratti, I am so relieved now. I will be here for you. What do you want me to do?'

'I know you have a son. Where is he? I need someone to support us from outside. We cannot go against Surya directly. This has to happen behind the scenes. He is going to Pala tomorrow, and we need to act quickly. Maybe we can capture him along the way, but I need people.'

'Thampratti, my son is only an adolescent. I do not think he would be capable of doing this.'

Bhavani moved forward and held her hand. 'Trust me. We can do this. I just need a few people from outside to make this happen. Please let your son meet me. I will make sure he is safe through the entire process.'

She turned and walked back to house. Nanamma stood there, not knowing what to say.

The girl returned after giving food to Kelu. She smiled at Bhavani and nodded her head, acknowledging Kelu had enjoyed food.

Bhavani asked her to make a grand meal for lunch, with all the food Kelu loved when Mother was around.

Surya came into the kitchen and said, 'I think I should leave today so I can be back before the weekend. The temple festival will start soon and I need to be here for that.'

Before Bhavani could respond, he walked back in a hurry. She followed Surya to his room.

'Do you need anything for your journey, like food? My sister took care of you and I don't know your likes and dislikes.'

'No. I need nothing.' He turned and pulled her to in. 'I will miss you though. I cannot wait to love you. Why have you never shown this interest in me before?'

'When my sister was alive, I had to be respectful. Now, things have obviously changed.' She turned to the door, her face stiff with anger.

Surya watched her walk away, admiring her beauty and the rhythm of her walk.

The next day, Bhavani got up very early. She had one week to plan and execute. She ran to the outbuilding. Kelu seemed a little better. She told him her plan, and Kelu said he could get this done with his people.

Bhavani stopped him. 'You better stay here. If we do something, we need to do it without your involvement. I want this done with no suspicion on us. But he needs to suffer for months, and I need a place for that. Do you have any location?'

'Yes. The warehouse in Pala. I have safely placed many low-caste women there, and no one will suspect anything. You cannot find a better place than that. You can get Kannan to show you.'

'Pala is good, but I cannot go talk to Kannan now. Not with Surya there.'

'Send the workers who you know the best. They can convey the message without Surya knowing. Can you trust anyone here?' Kelu asked.

'Yes. Nanamma and her son'

'Then send them both. They can do this. They will blend in. Make sure you send the message in writing with our seal. Otherwise, Kannan will not believe them. Tell Kannan I am in danger. He will rise to the occasion. Surya is no match to him. I can't wait to spit in his face. He will see my other side, the side only a few people have ever seen.'

Kelu exhaled deeply in relief and hugged Bhavani.

She said, 'Wait for the good news, Father. I am leaving now, and I will not come back until Surya is captive in the warehouse.'

Bhavani left and Kelu paced with excitement. He could not wait to see Surya in pain. Now and then Kelu hit the wall with his fist. Psyching himself, he jumped up and down.

Bhavani ran back to the house and found Nanamma. 'Where is your son?'

'Thampratti, please don't ask my son to do anything. I have only him. He is very young.'

'Nanamma, it's okay. You are going with him and I don't want him to fight or anything. I just need you to go to Pala and give a letter to Kannan. Then stay there until you see me again. Is that clear?'

Nanamma approached the farm with a determined stride, her mind focused on the task ahead. Her son, Neelan, was busy ploughing the soil, his brow glistening with sweat under the morning sun.

At seventeen, Neelan was sturdy and strong, with a wiry frame honed by years of hard labour. His skin was sun-darkened, and his eyes held a mixture of curiosity and earnestness that reflected his determination.

His clothes were simple but clean, and he moved with a confidence born from the hard work he had always known.

Neelan glanced up, surprised to see his mother arriving so early. She usually brought lunch, not news of urgent tasks.

'Is everything okay, Mother?' he asked, concern etched into his voice.

Nanamma, catching her breath, looked at her son with a mixture of pride and apprehension. 'Thampratti wants us to travel to Pala with a job. It is a little dangerous for us.'

Neelan's eyes widened slightly as he absorbed the weight of his mother's words. He set aside the plow and wiped his hands on his simple cloth. His expression turned thoughtful, but soon a resolute smile spread across his face.

'Don't worry, Mother,' he said with a firm voice that belied his youth. 'Kannan Thampra will take care of everything. We are just delivering the message. Yes, we have to be careful, but we need to support Thampratti. Her mother gave us this life we enjoy now. Otherwise, we would have rotted in our old village with our abusive father and the society's higher-ups. Here, no one bothers us, and we get food, good clothing, and a job every day. I am honoured to help Thampratti. Let's go.'

Neelan's confidence was reassuring. He had grown up in hardship, and it had forged in him a resilience and a sense of honour that guided his actions.

The prospect of supporting Thampratti, who had offered them a chance at a better life, was an opportunity he embraced wholeheartedly. His words were not just a reassurance to his mother but a reflection of his own deep gratitude and unwavering loyalty.

With that, Neelan gathered his things, ready to accompany his mother on the journey. His resolve and the understanding of the importance of their mission gave him strength.

As they set off, his determination was a bright spark amid the uncertainty, lighting their path with hope and purpose.

They went to the shack nearby the farm where they lived. Kelu and his men had helped Neelan put together the shack a few months back. It was nothing much, but they were both content.

They changed from their work clothes to the somewhat decent ones they had. Nanamma looked at her boy. He was growing to be a sturdy young man. Hard work on the farm was making him strong. He was actually the same age as Bhavani. Nanamma often forgot that her only son was really a man now.

In the main house, Bhavani sat down at her father's desk. She took few palm leaves to write the message.

It could not be too long, yet Kannan needed to know what had happened. She scribbled and tears flowed. She couldn't believe how much she changed. She never thought she would be this emotional.

But circumstances changed people, and she was now living that reality. Everyone saw her as her father's daughter, but her mother had been everything to her. The void she felt after her death was unbearable.

'Thampratti.'

Bhavani jumped out of her deep thoughts. She rose from her chair and walked to the verandah. Nanamma and Neelan were there, ready to go. Their attire was not apt for traveling this far, so Bhavani gave them some nice clothes.

'And you are not going to walk all that way. You will take the bullock cart from here. Closer to Pala, stop the cart and then walk the remaining distance to town. Stay low key, and if you see Surya, stay away from him. If he sees you, he may get suspicious. Neelan, you may need to help Kannan. He may not have enough bodies. Regardless, this mission needs to be successful. Is that clear?'

'Yes, Thampratti. We will do this carefully.'

Bhavani watched them walk away. They readied the cart Kelu used all the time. Bhavani rushed into the kitchen, packed some food for them, and ran back out. She caught them before the cart left the compound.

Nanamma smiled at Bhavani. 'Thampratti, we do this for your mother. She lived for us all her life.'

Bhavani moved forward and hugged her. They stayed like that for a while. Life had taken a huge toll on them in the past few days.

Finally, Neelan hit the bullock with his stick, signalling the urgency. They left for Pala.

The sun was slowly taking its path to hide for the night, and Bhavani walked toward the land where her sister and mother had been cremated. The soil was black and the pyre was still a little hot. She felt their hearts burning in there. Both had a lot of life ahead, yet God planned something else for them. They both were nicer than me, yet they got the punishment. Life was strange.

Bhavani returned to the house. This time, she had no tears on her walk. She felt the plan was on the move and would succeed.

Suddenly, she realized she had not sent food for Kelu in the afternoon. She rushed back to kitchen. The girl who worked in the kitchen was sitting by the cooking pit.

She said, 'Thampratti, Kelu Thampra loved the afternoon food.' Bhavani felt relieved. She hugged the girl and said, 'I got worried. I forgot about my father, but you did it for me. Thank you so much.'

'Thampratti, I saw what happened and I want Surya Thampra to pay the price. Don't you worry about your father. I will take care of his food.'

Bhavani thanked her again and then went to her room. She went to bed right away.

Her body was tired and her mind was not working properly anymore. She sank into the valley of unconsciousness.

'Bhavani.'

'Mother? You look so beautiful.'

'Daughter, I am proud of you what you do now. But be careful. Your anger gets you to respond without thinking. I love you so much.'

Bhavani shot up in bed. 'Mother?' She cried once she realized it was a dream only. She couldn't sleep after that.

***

Nanamma and Neelan reached Pala the following afternoon. They walked around the town just to study the circumstances. Everything seemed as usual. They walked past the shop Kannan ran.

Inside, they saw Surya sitting by the till. Kannan was not there. They crossed the road and waited behind the shack used for holding water for travellers.

Hours passed, but Kannan never showed up and Surya never left.

Neelan jumped when someone touched his shoulder from behind.

'I know you,' Kannan said. 'You are from Kelu uncle's house. Why are you here? Come to the shop and we can talk there.'

'No, Thampra. We need to give you something and go. Surya Thampra should know nothing about this. Bhavani Thampratti gave us this letter for you.'

Kannan took the letter with some hesitation and they all went farther down the road to a place where there was a farm. They all sat as Kannan read the letter.

Kannan couldn't comprehend how everything had unravelled so quickly. His thoughts were filled with confusion and anger.

How had Surya managed to manipulate all of them so easily? It was a question that gnawed at him, intensifying his sense of betrayal and helplessness.

His mind flashed back to the days when his father was alive, and how Kelu uncle had stepped in as a pillar of support after his father's death. He owed so much to that family, a debt that went beyond mere gratitude.

The thought of Surya's treachery made his blood boil, especially knowing the pain and suffering it had caused to Narayani and Lakshmi aunty.

His heart ached for Narayani, who had always been a gentle, nurturing presence in his life, and for Lakshmi aunty, whose strength and resilience had inspired him countless times.

The devastation Surya had brought upon them was unforgivable. He felt a fierce determination rise within him, a resolve to protect what was left of his family and honour the memory of those they had lost.

He sat there and cried a bit.

Once he had composed himself, Kannan arranged a place for them to stay overnight. He advised them lay low. He would send them food and a change of clothes. He also advised them that the plan may not work right away. He needed to figure out manpower.

Back in the store, Surya was waiting for Kannan. He was upset. 'Is this how you run the shop? All day you did not come here. How do you account for all the sales? What if the employees steal all the money while you are gone?'

Kannan stopped him. 'Surya, I am not answerable to you. I am running this business better than my father did, and Kelu uncle knows that. I am not even reporting back to Uncle anymore. This is my business and I run however I want. Please don't create unnecessary problems.'

Kannan walked inside without waiting for a response.

Surya was seething with anger. He pushed over the cashier's table, spilling all the coins on the floor.

The employees and clients in the store couldn't believe what had just happened. Hearing the commotion, Kannan felt this was the right time. The town would back him up and there may be no other opportunity.

Kannan rushed back out and screamed, 'Get that guy! How dare he trash my store?'

The employees all approached Surya. He got up quickly and pulled out a knife.

'Move away from me! I will cut anyone who touches me.' He swung his knife and walked backward toward the exit. The employees followed him out.

'Don't let him escape,' Kannan yelled.

People from neighbouring shops came out. They all knew Kannan, but Surya had never come to Pala so he was an unfamiliar face. He was outnumbered quickly.

People from all over surrounded him. Surya knew he had no choice but to surrender. They tied his hands and put him into Kannan's bullock cart.

'You are making a mistake,' Surya said. 'If Kelu knew about this, he would not spare you. I am his son-in-law.'

Kannan covered Surya's eyes and drove the cart forward. The road to the warehouse was bumpy. Surya felt very uneasy. He had never dealt with Kannan.

'What are you doing? Where are you taking me? If you stop this and let me go now, I will let nothing happen to you.'

Kannan did not say a word, and took the longest and the roughest route to the warehouse. After a time, Surya felt an abrupt halt.

His heart hammered in his chest. He could hear metal door or something squeaking. He tried to move his blindfold by rubbing his face on the cart's floor.

A powerful pull yanked him out of the cart and someone forced him to walk.

Kannan made Surya walk all the way around the warehouse several times, then he made Surya walk towards his left and then again left, stopped for a minute.

He shoved Surya, who stumbled and lost his balance. Kannan caught him and spun him around, then walked him all the way around the warehouse again a few more times before finally entering the building.

This gave Surya the impression that they had walked a long distance from the road to get to this place. Kannan knew Surya never had come here before.

He pushed Surya into a small chamber with a steel door. There were no windows. Dim light came from a dirty glass tile high in the ceiling. Olden days, the chamber was used to store grain.

Kannan said, 'You will live here till you die. I know what you did to my sister Narayani and my aunt.'

Surya couldn't believe what he'd heard. 'What are you saying? What do you think I did? I think you got the wrong information. Who said this to you?'

Kannan pulled off Surya's blindfold and slapped him so hard Surya lost his balance and fell.

'Don't you dare speak a word! Bhavani will decide your fate.'

Surya struggled to get up with his hands tied. Kannan kicked him in the ribs. Surya screamed for help.

'No one will come to help you. You think it's that easy to take everything from Uncle, and you come here to take my business too?'

'You will learn a lesson,' Surya shrieked. 'If you kill me, Bhavani will kill you. She is now my wife. You may not know, but Bhavani is in on my plan. She loved when I put Kelu in prison. She was the one who sent me here to take over your business.'

Kannan slapped him again. 'Don't! You want to live, keep quiet. We will give you food and water, but this room is your world now. You open your dirty mouth again, and I will carve your tongue out.'

Kannan walked out and locked the chamber.

'I hate darkness. I need a lamp in here,' Surya yelled,

'Get used to it, Surya,' Kannan replied coldly as he walked away.

***

Author's Note

As a writer, I am a firm believer in destiny and fate. While some may debate whether destiny and fate are synonymous, my journey with this book leans more towards fate. It's intriguing to note that both this book and my previous work, 'Droplets,' began on the same significant day in the Hindu calendar, the first day of Ramayan.

In South India, this month-long reading of the Ramayan is revered for its cleansing and auspicious qualities, symbolizing the pursuit of good over evil. This alignment further strengthens my belief in fate— two separate creations starting on the same day.

One of the most remarkable aspects of this writing journey was creating the character Bhavani. She emerged as the strong matriarch of the main family in this story, embodying qualities of resilience and action over mere rhetoric. In a world where discussions about equality often dominate, Bhavani serves as a powerful example of someone who stands out through her deeds rather than words.

Bhavani's character resonates deeply with women who face daily struggles and societal pressures. She becomes a beacon of hope for those crushed under societal expectations, illustrating resilience and the ability to rise above adversity.

Additionally, Bhavani challenges those who seemingly have it all yet find themselves unhappy, offering a perspective on what true fulfilment entails.

The process of creating Bhavani has been transformative for me personally. During challenging times, I found strength in contemplating how Bhavani would confront adversity with unwavering positivity. Her resilience and determination became a guiding light, reinforcing my commitment to infuse positivity into my storytelling.

Ultimately, my goal in sharing Bhavani's story was to inspire and uplift others. If my writing can spark inspiration and resonate with readers, then I believe I have fulfilled my mission as a writer.

Acknowledgments

This novel is a tribute to the extraordinary women who have fought relentlessly to challenge societal norms and create lasting change. To those who refused to back down simply because they were women, you are the backbone of our community.

There's a saying: *Teach a woman, and she will teach the village; teach a man, and he will care only for himself.*

This story is a heartfelt acknowledgment of the resilience, courage, and unyielding spirit of women who have dared to fight against injustice. I am profoundly grateful to have been shaped by the remarkable women in my life.

To my mother, whose unwavering strength ensured her siblings thrived while she selflessly nurtured her own family.

To my great-grandmother, who stood tall and fearless, protecting her grandchildren and defending her legacy even when her own people sought to dismantle it.

And to my wife, who inspires me every day with her wisdom, compassion, and leadership, guiding me to navigate this complex world with purpose and grace.

I am also deeply thankful for the blessings and support I have received over the years. To my teachers, whose guidance lit my path; my friends, who stood by me through every challenge; my children, who bring joy and inspiration to my life.

I am deeply grateful to Dalbir Singh, Mohit Gupta, Naseer and the entire team of Tridev Publishers for their remarkable efforts. Your unwavering faith in me has been both an inspiration and a driving force throughout this journey.

To all those who have been a part of my story, directly or indirectly, thank you for your unwavering support and encouragement. This novel is as much yours as it is mine.